"I don't want to date just anyone. The only one I'd love to take out is you. From the moment you came here, it's all I've wanted."

She wanted to give in to the joy of hearing those words, but her reality wouldn't allow it.

"I don't know who you think I am, but I'm telling you that if you just got to know me a little more, you would see that you wouldn't want a woman like me."

"I know you, whether you want to admit it or not."

She gave a sardonic chuckle. "Just because we've been passing each other on the ranch since I got here doesn't mean you know me. You have merely seen me. We have fundamental differences. Number one—you have more dates than a fruitcake. I don't want a man whose attention I have to struggle to keep."

"Unless we go out, how do you know if we have fundamental differences?" He leaned against the chair closest to him. "And, wait...does fruitcake even have dates in it?"

Acknowledgments

This series wouldn't have been possible without a great team of people, including my editors at Harlequin—thank you for all your hard work.

Also, thank you to Suzanne Miller and the crew at Dunrovin Ranch in Lolo, Montana. Suzanne is the inspiration behind one of my favorite characters in this series, the fantastic Eloise Fitzgerald. Just like Eloise, she always greets you with a warm smile and an open heart.

MR. TAKEN

———

DANICA WINTERS

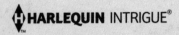

HARLEQUIN INTRIGUE®

To Mac,

From sea to shining sea, it will always and forever be you and me.

Thanks for making life such an amazing adventure.

ISBN-13: 978-1-335-72135-8

Recycling programs
for this product may
not exist in your area.

Mr. Taken

Copyright © 2017 by Danica Winters

This edition published by arrangement with Harlequin Books S.A.

For questions and comments about the quality of this book, please contact us at CustomerService@Harlequin.com.

® and TM are trademarks of Harlequin Enterprises Limited or its corporate affiliates. Trademarks indicated with ® are registered in the United States Patent and Trademark Office, the Canadian Intellectual Property Office and in other countries.

Printed in U.S.A.

www.Harlequin.com

Danica Winters is a multiple award-winning, bestselling author who writes books that grip readers with their ability to drive emotion through suspense and occasionally a touch of magic. When she's not working, she can be found in the wilds of Montana, testing her patience while she tries to hone her skills at various crafts—quilting, pottery and painting are not her areas of expertise. She believes the cup is neither half-full nor half-empty, but it better be filled with wine. Visit her website at danicawinters.net.

Books by Danica Winters

Harlequin Intrigue

Mystery Christmas

Ms. Calculation
Mr. Serious
Mr. Taken

Smoke and Ashes
Dust Up with the Detective
Wild Montana

Visit the Author Profile page at Harlequin.com.

CAST OF CHARACTERS

Whitney Barstow—This cowgirl is taking no chances after her life was nearly ended by her ex-husband when he set fire to her family's barn. Out of fear for her family's safety and her own, she has taken to the road and found herself thousands of miles away from her home and working the front desk at Dunrovin Ranch.

Colter Fitzgerald—Charm should have been this firefighter's middle name. Everywhere he goes, the women of Mystery, Montana, swoon. Yet, he only has eyes for Whitney—the one woman who refuses to give him the time of day.

Wyatt Fitzgerald—Colter's brother and the local sheriff's deputy, who quickly finds himself neck-deep in an investigation that calls into question not only his detective skills, but a whole slew of his family's history.

Eloise Fitzgerald—Foster mother and caregiver not only to the people in her life but to the animals as well, she is the head matriarch of the Fitzgerald clan.

William Poe—A shady county tax appraiser who has a running feud with the Fitzgeralds, he thinks everyone and everything belongs to him—including the women of Mystery, Montana.

Daryl Bucket—A long-haul trucker who has come to the aid of the family in the past but now may have more tricks up his sleeve.

Sarah Rizzo—Owner of Pretties and Pastries, the local café that has been catering the Fitzgeralds' events, but Sarah hopes she can become even more involved with the family.

Frank Harris—On the run and potentially dangerous, Whitney's ex-husband may have finally located the runaway—and he may do whatever it takes to make sure she doesn't slip through his grasp once again.

Chapter One

No matter how hard Whitney Barstow tried, there was one memory that never seemed to fade or be twisted by time—it was the moment she had nearly died. The smoke had filled her lungs, stealing her oxygen and making her head ache. The acrid smoke was like hands covering her mouth and nose, and however hard she tried to breathe, they only clenched harder. She had torn at the invisible hands, leaving faint scars on her face—a personal reminder of her desperation to survive.

Every time she closed her eyes, she was back in the barn. The door was closed, and when the spark had hit the hay, it was like a bomb that had gone off. She could still hear the *whoomp* as the dry tinder erupted into flames. And the heat. Oh, the heat. Some nights she would wake up in a cold sweat, her body's reflexes kicking in at the mere thought of being trapped in the inferno once again.

A tear slipped down her cheek as she stared out at the barn that sat at the heart of Dunrovin Ranch, and her thoughts turned to the lives she'd lost. There would be no replacing Runs Like the Wind, her black Thoroughbred. She could still smell the scent of hay on the horse's breath and feel her smooth gait from high in the saddle. Nothing would ever be the same. There was no going back and stopping evil from entering her life. There was no undoing what had been done.

There was only one thing she could do to keep the memories at bay—she could never ride again.

Even now, almost ten years later, she could barely step foot in a barn. If she was forced, it was only if the door was kept open and the breeze drifted through like a promise of freedom. She couldn't be trapped again. Not by a person, and never by fire. Never.

"Whit, are you okay, sweetheart?" Mrs. Eloise Fitzgerald called out from the main office.

Whitney angrily wiped away the tear that had escaped. She didn't have room in her life for weakness—or vulnerability. It was emotional weakness that always got her into trouble. If she just stayed tough and shut the world out—even Mrs. Fitzgerald, the kindly matriarch of the Fitzgerald family—she would never have to worry about getting hurt again.

"I'm fine," she called back to her boss. "Just wanted a bit of fresh air before the guests started arriving for the weekend."

Mrs. Fitzgerald walked out onto the porch and wrapped her arms around her body, shielding herself from the bitter December air. "Brr... You are going to catch your death of cold out here if you don't get your skinny buns inside, little thing."

Whitney snorted a laugh. It would be ironic, dying by hypothermia after nearly dying by fire. "I don't mind the cold," she said with a smile she hoped would calm Eloise's nerves.

Eloise waved her inside, not letting her get away with such disregard for her well-being. "You know what I always say... *You don't have anything if you don't have your health.*"

Her health was just fine, thank you very much... It was the rest of Whitney that could really have used some work. She hadn't been on a date in two years, and her best friend was the ranch dog, Milo, that no one else seemed to notice. Some days, when the phones were not ringing and she found herself looking for work to do, it was almost as if she and the dog were really nothing more than apparitions.

She walked over to the fence and ran her finger over one of the red Christmas lights that were looped between the posts. Maybe she was just like the Ghost of Christmas Past, an enigma sent to warn others that if they were like her, and continued living set in their ways, only bad things were bound to happen.

Or maybe she was just spending entirely too much time alone, wrapped up in her head and the things that needed to be done around the place. Ever since the murders, everything had slowed down—guests weren't filing in and out as they once did, and even

their annual Yule Night celebration was barely getting off the ground. It was almost as if the deaths of
the women in and around the ranch were only a pre-
cursor of what was to come—like some dire warning that nothing could be warm and fuzzy, not even
during the holidays.

Maybe she really needed to talk, to lay bare her
feelings. Maybe she wasn't alone in her fears. And as
much as she dreaded opening up, if she was going to
communicate with anyone, Eloise would have been
a good choice. The woman had seen it all and ex-
perienced even more. She'd raised handfuls of kids
from all kinds of backgrounds, been through fam-
ine and hardship, and yet always seemed to have a
smile on her face and soup on the stove. She was
the epitome of perfection—always put together and
selfless when it came to those she cared for. And of
late, all her energies had been focused on looking
after the ranch and handling the uproar it had been
facing. Yet, even with all this, she had been making
time to come and see Whitney and ensure that she
was settling into her new role on the ranch.

"You need to come on in," Eloise called again, her
teeth chattering slightly as she spoke.

For the woman's benefit, she made her way over
to the door and stepped into her cramped office, and
Eloise followed. The place was overflowing with
books, and papers littered the desk in no discernible
order. She grimaced as she looked over at Eloise,

who was staring at the mess as though it was the first time she had taken notice.

"Sweetheart," Eloise started, "do you think it's possible that we could get a few of these things filed away?"

"Not a problem, ma'am." She set about shuffling the papers that sat on the farthest corner of the desk and shoving them in the already burgeoning bottom drawer of the desk. She tried to push it closed, but the drawer burped the extra copies of the ranch's tri-fold brochures and a notepad filled with scrawled notes.

She laughed as she turned around and tried to hide the mess behind her.

Eloise smiled, ever elegant and kind even in the face of inadequacy. "Do you want me to show you how I would organize all this?"

Whitney loved how the woman didn't try to force her through guilt, but rather the gentle and practiced hand of patience; yet she wasn't the kind to accept acts of pity. "I think I can—"

Thankfully, there was the harsh ding of the bell at the front desk and it saved Whitney from having to ask for help. She could handle the responsibilities of the front office. In truth, the mess had diminished in size since last week, but she was sure Eloise wasn't ready to hear that though her office was a disaster, it was cleaner than it had been in nearly a month.

As she walked out the door toward the parlor where they received guests, she was stopped when she ran into a man. Well, not any man, but Colter. The well-muscled, ridiculously handsome Fitzgerald brother who was nearly as reclusive as she. "Oh, hey, sorry. I didn't mean to—" She took a step back from him as she realized she was so close to him that she could smell the traces of smoke on his skin even though it was masked by the heady aroma of his cologne.

It struck her that no matter how many showers a person could take or how much perfume he used to cover up the smell of a fire, it wasn't something that could be fully erased—just like her memory, it had a way of nearly permeating into a person all the way to the soul. Or maybe it was just the fact that she knew what he did for a living, the risks he took and the panic he had to face each and every day, which brought the scent back to the front of her mind. It was almost like one of Pavlov's dogs except firefighter equaled smoke, and smoke equaled...fear.

She took another step back. Though he was one sexy hunk of man, with his dark black cowboy hat and whiskey-colored eyes, he was the living embodiment of danger.

"You're fine," he said, a giant, almost comically large grin on his face. "But you know if you wanted to touch my body, all you had to do was ask."

"Ugh. You really are full of yourself. Aren't you, Colter?" She couldn't help the heat that rose in her cheeks as he teased her. It wasn't that she hadn't imagined running her fingers over the lines of the muscles that adorned his chest. Every staff member at the ranch had a fantasy about at least one of the

Fitzgerald brothers—who, of late, had been getting scooped up by women prettier and far more accomplished than her.

"I've been called full of something, but it ain't usually myself," he said, his Montana drawl kicking into an even higher gear than his smile.

"Well, if no one has had the guts to call you on it, then I'm more than happy to step up to the plate. You, Mr. Colter Fitzgerald, aren't God's gift to women. In fact, in case you didn't know, you are the last man I would ever think about dating. I'd rather date…" She paused as she tried to come up with a man in place of him, but none came to mind. As the seconds ticked by, her heart rate climbed. He couldn't see her like this. She had to be cool, calm, collected and, above all, witty—and she had nothing.

"You'd rather date whom?" he asked, with that all-too-cute grin and a wiggle of the eyebrow.

"Dang it, you know what I mean… I would rather date anyone than you."

"As long as it's no one else in particular, I think I like my odds." He laughed, the sound as rich and full of depth as his eyes.

She groaned, but the sound didn't take on the edge of real annoyance like she had wanted it to; in fact, to her ears it almost sounded like the awful noise a woman made when she was trying not to fall for a man. And she was definitely, absolutely, categorically never going to fall for the infamous jokester Colter Fitzgerald. Nope. Not gonna happen. She would never let him win her over as long as she stayed in her right mind. Not that she had a left mind, but... well... She sighed.

No.

The bell tinged to life again from the parlor, reminding her of the guests who were undoubtedly growing more impatient by the second with her absence.

"Excuse me—I have work to do. Unlike some of us," she said under her breath as she pushed past him, careful not to touch him again.

His laughter followed her into the parlor until she shut the door to drown him out. The last thing she needed to do was spend a moment thinking about that man.

Standing at the front desk was a man and a woman. They looked to be in their midthirties, and based on the woman's coiffed hair, to-the-sky black stilettos, and brown Louis Vuitton purse, they were definitely among their elite clientele. They had probably come here to spend their trust-fund money on some idealistic and romantic getaway that involved a horse-drawn sleigh and a bearskin rug in front of the crackling fireplace.

The woman was carrying what looked to be a slightly oversize fur ball, or maybe it was just one of those New York rats everyone talked about. Yet, as Whitney drew closer walking to the desk, the rat-looking creature picked up its ears and growled. Dog. Definitely a dog. It probably had one of those stupid names like Fifi or

Fredrico. It was funny, but most of their elite guests had a dog just like that one, an accessory to their outfit—but most were cuter than the one this particular woman held.

"How may I help you folks?" Whitney said, using her practiced service-industry charm.

"It took you long enough," the woman said, nearly spitting the words.

"Dear, I'm sure she was busy," the man said, patting the woman lightly on the hand and drawing Whitney's attention to the massive diamond that adorned the woman's ring finger.

For a moment she wondered if they had drawn her attention to it on purpose, some well-practiced motion that drew even more attention to their status and wealth. Whitney forced herself to smile just a little bit brighter, but the truth in Montana was simple— no one really cared about how much money anyone had or the number of things a person owned. Respect and honor were only given to those whose character merited such accolades. It was one of the reasons she had picked this state as her home instead of staying in Kentucky.

"I don't care if she was busy or not. We have flown halfway around the country to be here. The least she could do is be present when we arrive," the woman said, continuing her rampage.

Whitney bit her tongue instead of telling the woman that Dunrovin Ranch was a beautiful and majestic place, but it was a long way from the Four Seasons. If the woman had wanted to be catered to hand and foot, she should have picked a resort that would have done that—and not come to a guest ranch.

"If you like," Whitney said, forcing herself to behave, "and are interested in relaxing, there is a spa about ten miles back down the road. I can set up an appointment for you."

"Ten miles? Where are we, on the back side of Hell?" The woman glared at her husband, who must have been the one to book their trip.

The man smiled at Whitney, clearly embarrassed by his wife's atrocious behavior. "Is there any way we could have the masseuse come here?"

"I'll see what I can do," Whitney said, though she was fully aware the local masseuse, Jess Lewis, would throw a holy hissy fit at the request. Yet if they gave her a few extra bucks she would quiet down in no time.

She took down the couple's names and got them the keys to their room—the nicest private cabin at the ranch, a two-story, nearly three-thousand-square-foot log home with marble and leather everywhere. "Let me know if there's anything further I can assist you with," Whitney said, the forced niceties like sand on her tongue.

"Actually," the woman said, handing over the rat creature, "I don't want Francesca to be a bother to me this weekend. I need you to handle her."

Whitney balked at the woman as she stuffed the dog into her hands.

Handle her? The last thing on her long list of duties was dog handler or kennel master. Whitney had work to do. She slowly lowered the dog to the floor behind the desk. "I... Uh..." she stammered.

"That's great. Perfect," the woman continued, clearly not used to her requests being denied no matter how asinine they might have been.

The man opened the door and waited as his wife pranced out, her stilettos clicking on the floor like the shrill impatient cadence of fingers. Whitney just stared at the computer screen for a moment as she reminded herself these kinds of people played a big part in why she had left her home state, and she took some level of comfort in the fact that they were outsiders and going to leave just as quickly as they came.

A cold wind kicked up and spilled through the door, whipping dry fragile snowflakes onto the guest book that sat at the side of the desk. She walked over and touched the door. As she looked outside, running toward the entrance of the roundabout driveway was the little rat creature. Its dark fur sat stark against the snow as it sprinted toward freedom. She stood still for a moment, letting it get away. With an owner like hers, the dog deserved to have one go at escaping.

On the other hand, Whitney would have to answer to said owners, and she could only imagine their response if the dog was actually lost. No matter how softhearted Eloise was, Whitney would probably lose her job, and therefore her room at the ranch. She would have to start all over.

This dog's freedom wasn't worth it.

What was the dog's name again? "Fifi!" she called, but the dog didn't slow down. "Fredrico!" Again, the dog simply kept running. She ran out the door, her cowboy boots thumping on the wooden porch as she made her way to the driveway. "Lassie, come home!" she cried again.

There was the boom of laughter from behind her. She turned to see Colter watching her. "Did Timmy fall in the well again?"

"Really?" she scoffed. "If you're not going to go after the dog, at least you can be quiet."

His laughter lightened, but he didn't stop chuckling. "All right, all right. I'll come to little Lassie's rescue. Where did she go?"

She turned back and looked out at the driveway. A '90s blue Dodge truck was rumbling down the road toward them.

"No. Stop!" she screamed at the truck, almost as though the driver could hear her through the closed windows and the crunch of gravel under the tires. The man driving didn't even seem to see her.

He barreled down the road. Just as he was about to cross over the steel cattle guard, the little rat creature ran out. It wove in front of the truck, stopping as it stared up at the blue beast careening toward it.

"No!" Whitney yelled.

The dog took off running toward the truck. Just as they were about to collide, the dog slipped between the bars of the cattle guard that stretched across the end of the driveway, and disappeared. It wasn't Timmy or the well, but it looked like they would have to pull off their own version of a rescue.

Chapter Two

He'd been at the save-a-life game for a long time now, but this was the first time Colter Fitzgerald had to save a dog from the jaws of a cattle guard. He waved at the guy driving the truck, motioning for him to go ahead. The guy had dark, oily hair that sparkled in the winter sun. Sitting on the man's dashboard was a wooden bat, and the sight made chills ripple down Colter's spine.

In a split second, everything could have really gone downhill. The driver's grim face and demeanor were far from friendly. So much so, Colter was thankful he had not climbed down to confront them about the dog that had appeared from nowhere in front of his vehicle. He watched in relief as the trucker drove past them with a curt wave and the taillights vanished in the distance. The last thing he needed, especially in his quest to impress Whitney, was a run-in with a hard-edged stranger.

Whitney Barstow hadn't been his mother's employee for very long. From his recollection, it had been exactly three months since she set foot on his mother's porch and asked for any job that didn't involve the care and maintenance of horses. At the time, he had thought it was odd anyone would want to come to a ranch and not work with the animals, but he had let it go—everyone had their quirks. Besides, every time he caught a glimpse of her gray eyes, they made him nearly forget his name, not to mention any of her faults. To him, she was perfect, even the way she seemed to be constantly annoyed by him.

He glanced over at her as she stared into the grates of the cattle guard. "It's okay, sweet puppy. We're going to get you out. Don't worry," she cooed, her voice taking on the same soft edge she must have used with small children.

Colter smiled as she looked up at him and the sunlight caught in her hair and made it shine like each strand was spun out of gold. "What are we going to do?" she asked, motioning toward the grate.

The steel bars had been bent, apparently just enough for a small pooch to fall between. Yet instead of staying where they could simply pull it, the dog had wedged itself deep into the corner of the trough beneath. The pup shook as it stood on the collection of cracked ice and looked up at them, its eyes rimmed with white. It had to have been cold down there, and the poor creature was ill-prepared, with its short hair and low body fat, to withstand frigid temperatures for long. They'd have to act fast.

He stood up and rushed toward the barn. "I'll grab the tractor," he called over his shoulder.

She nodded but turned back to the dog. "Come here, baby."

He didn't know a great deal about the little animal that looked like a Chihuahua, but he did know that no amount of calling was going to get that dog to come to her. A dog like that was notorious for being a one-person animal. According to one guest he'd talked to, who had owned a similar dog, that was the allure—to have an animal that fawned over only its owner. It was like owning the cat of the dog world.

The barn doors gave a loud grind of metal on metal as he slid them open. He took in a deep breath. He loved the smell of animals almost as much as he loved the animals themselves. Most people might have found the scent of feed, sweat and grime too much, but for a firefighter like him, it was the perfume of life—and it reminded him how lucky he was to have the opportunity to live it. It wasn't like the smell of ash. He'd read poem after poem that likened the scent of ash to renewal, but it never drew images of a phoenix to his mind; rather, it only reminded him of the feeling of what it was to lose and be destroyed from the inside out.

He grabbed a steel chain and the keys that hung on the wall just inside the door, and made his way back outside to the tractor parked just under the overhang.

The tractor started with a chug and a sputter. The old beast fought hard to start, thanks to the cold, but it had been through a lot. He pressed it forward and moved it out of its parking spot by the barn. The vehicle made groans and grumbles that sounded like promises of many more years of service. His parents had done a good job with the place, always setting everything up to last not just their lifetime, but for generations to come. It was hard to imagine that his parents used to have a life before—lives that didn't revolve around the comings and goings of the ranch, its guests and the foster kids who had passed in and out of their doors.

They had spent their lives giving everything they had to this place. He could have said the same things about his intention as a firefighter; he undoubtedly would give everything he had to his job, and the lives he would affect, but it wasn't the same. His job and lifestyle were finite. As soon as his body gave out and he was no longer physically able to do the job, someone new, younger would come in and take his place. In fact, as soon as he walked out of the station's doors, it would be like he had never really been there at all— likely only the people whose lives he'd touched would have any lasting thoughts of him.

He blew a warm breath of air onto his chilling fingers as he drove the tractor around the corner and onto the driveway. Maybe he was wrong in thinking that he had nothing in common with the phoenix. Maybe he had simply already risen from the ashes of a firefighter who had served before him, and when he aged out, another would take his place to renew their battalion.

The thought didn't upset him—it was an unspoken reality of their lifestyle—but when compared to his parents' lifestyle he couldn't help wondering if he had made the wrong choice. In all reality, he had only ever pulled one person out of a burning building, and it had been the town drunk after he had passed out with a cigarette listing from his lips. Most of his calls were accidents on the highway, grass fires and medical emergencies. If he had stayed on the ranch, he could have helped build the place up and worked on creating a legacy for his family for generations to come. As it was, none of his brothers had ever spoken of what would come.

What would come. Even with the roar of the tractor's engine, the words echoed within him. If things continued going as they had been doing over the last few months, there wouldn't be anything left to worry about. Reservations for the upcoming month had been tapering off rapidly. If they didn't turn things around, by next summer they would be unable to support the overhead it took to keep the ranch up and running.

He hated being the pessimistic type, so he tried to push aside his concerns. Things were never as bad as they appeared. For him, it always seemed like things had a way of working out. Hopefully the same could be said for the ranch. At least this month they had Yule Night.

Maybe if Yule Night went especially well, it could lighten some of his parents' burden. The last thing they needed after the murders was money troubles. It wasn't his job, but he would do everything in his power to make sure that the ranch would stay afloat—especially if that meant he could save puppies and look every part of a hero to the one woman he wanted to like him.

Whitney stood up and waved him to bring the tractor closer. She really was incredibly beautiful. She stretched, moving her shoulders back as she pressed her hands against her hips. As he looked at where her hands touched her round curves, he wished those hands could be his. It would be incredible to feel the touch of her skin, to run his fingers down the round arch of her hips and over the strong muscles that adorned her thighs.

She was so strong. Not just physically, but emotionally, as well. In fact, she had always made a point of being so strong that he barely knew anything about her past. She kept things so close to her chest that he longed to know more, to get her to trust him enough that she would open up. As it was, all he knew about her was that she had originally been from Kentucky—but that was only thanks to the fact that he had managed to catch a quick glimpse of her application on his mother's desk before she was hired.

Why was she so closed off? For a moment he wondered if she was hiding from something or someone, or if it was more that she was hiding something from them. No one came to nowhere, Montana, and hid on a ranch unless there was something in their lives, or in their past, that they were running away from.

Maybe one day, if he was lucky, she would open up to him. Though, just because everything seemed to work out in the end for him, he'd never call himself lucky—and that would be exactly what it would take to make Whitney think of him as anything more than just another source of annoyance.

"What took you so long?" she asked as he climbed down from the tractor and laid the chains over his shoulder.

He didn't know what was worse: the heaviness of the chains that dug into his skin or the disgust that tore through him from her gaze. He hadn't been gone more than a couple of minutes, yet he understood more than anyone that when there was an emergency, time seemed to slow down. Minutes turned into millennia, and those were the kinds of minutes which had a way of driving a person to madness.

He smiled, hoping some of the contempt she must have been feeling for him would dissipate. "I guess I could have put the tractor in third gear, but the way I see it, that dog ain't going nowhere."

She shook her head and turned away from him. Yeah, she hated him. She looked back and reached out. "Hand me the chain. We need to get the dog out of here before it gets hypothermic."

"Here," he said, handing her one end of the chain. "Hook this to the tractor's bucket. I'll get the guard."

She took the chain and did as he instructed while he made his way over to the cattle guard and peered in at the little dog. It looked up at him and whimpered. The sound made his gut ache and he wrapped the chain around the steel so that when he raised the bucket on the machine, it would lift the gate straight up and away from the dog. He'd have to be careful to avoid hurting the animal. Something like this could get a little hairy. One little slip, one weak link in the chain, and everything could go to hell in a handbasket in just a few seconds.

He secured the chain and made his way back to the tractor. In one smooth, slow motion he raised the tractor's bucket. The chain clinked and pulled taut, and he motioned to Whitney. "Ready?"

She gave him a thumbs-up.

He lifted the bucket higher, and the tractor shifted slightly as it fought to bring up the heavy grate that was frozen to the ground. With a pop of ice and the metallic twang, the grate pried loose from the concrete and the tractor hoisted it into the air. He rolled the machine back a few feet, just to be safe in case the chain broke. No one would get hurt, not on his watch.

He ran over to the dog and lifted it up from its den of ice. The pup was shivering and panting with fear. He ran his fingers down the animal, trying to reassure the terrified creature.

Whitney stood beside him and looked at him for a moment and smiled. There was an unexpected warmth in her eyes as she looked at him and then down at the dog. As he sent her a soft smile, she looked away—almost too quickly, as though she was avoiding his gaze. She reached down and opened up the buttons of her Western-style red shirt. "Here, let me have her," she said, motioning for the animal.

"You're a good dog," he said, handing her over to Whitney.

Ever so carefully, as though she were handling a fragile Fabergé egg, she moved the dog against her skin; but not before he caught a glimpse of her red bra, a red that perfectly matched the color of her plaid shirt. His mind instinctively moved to thoughts of what rested beneath her jeans. She was probably the kind of woman who always wore matching underwear. He closed his eyes as the image of her standing in front of him in only her lingerie flashed through his mind. His body coursed to life.

It was just lust. That was all this was. Or maybe it was just that she seemed so far out of his league that he couldn't help wanting her.

"Hey," she said, pulling him from his thoughts.

"Hmm?" he asked, trying to look at anything but the little spot of exposed flesh of her stomach just above the dog where, if she moved just right, he was sure he could have seen more of her forbidden bra.

"Want a beer?" She pointed to something resting in the snow not far from the other side of the cattle guard.

He jumped over the gaping trench and leaned

down to take a closer look. There, sitting in the fresh snow, was a green glass Heineken bottle. Jammed into the opening was a cloth, and inside was liquid. Picking it up, he pulled the cloth out and took a quick sniff. The pungent, chemical-laced aroma of gas cut through his senses like a knife.

He stuffed the rag back into the bottle and stared at the thing in his hand for a moment as Whitney came over to stand by his side.

He shouldn't have touched it. He never should have picked the dang thing up. Now his fingerprints were all over it.

"What is it?" she asked.

He glanced over at her and contemplated telling her the truth, but he didn't want to get her upset over something that may turn out to be nothing. Yet he couldn't keep the truth from her forever. It couldn't be helped.

"Unfortunately, it ain't beer," he said, lifting it a bit higher. "What it *is* is what we call a Molotov cocktail."

Her jaw dropped and she moved to grab it, but he pulled it away. If he was right, her fingerprints didn't need to be anywhere near this thing.

"You can't be serious. Why…? Who?" She stared at the bottle, but let her hands drop to her sides.

His thoughts moved to the guy in the blue truck. He hadn't seen the man drop anything out of the window, but that bottle hadn't been there long. Or maybe Colter was wrong and someone else had come, chickened out and left the flammable grenade as a warning.

Either way, it looked as though someone had planned to act against the ranch. More, someone had wanted to hurt the place and the ones he loved.

Chapter Three

Whitney wasn't the kind who got scared easily, but seeing that bottle in Colter's hand had made every hair on her body stand on end. There were any number of people, thanks to the news of the deaths and the kidnapping, who had a bone to pick with Dunrovin; yet it just didn't make sense to her that someone would come here with the intention of making things worse. Why throw a bomb? Why harm those who worked here? None of the people who currently worked or lived on the ranch were guilty of any wrongdoing.

Well, at least any wrongdoing when it came to the ranch. She couldn't think about her past, not when it came to this. She bit the inside of her cheek as she mindlessly petted the dog that was safely tucked into her shirt.

"Do you think we should call the police?" she asked, tilting her chin in the direction of the dangerous object.

Colter sighed. "We probably should, but I'm not sure that having any more police out to the ranch is

a great idea right now. Maybe this is nothing. Maybe
it was just something someone had in the back of
their pickup and it just bounced out as they drove
over the cattle guard. Maybe it's just spare gas or
something, you know."

His feeble attempt to make her feel better didn't
work. She could hear the lie in his voice. They both
knew all too well this wasn't just some innocuous
thing. This was someone's failed effort to cause damage.

Yet to a certain degree she agreed with him. The
last thing the place needed was more negative press.
Even though his brother Wyatt was a deputy for the
local sheriff's office, it didn't mean they would be
able to keep this thing under wraps. If they called
911, everyone in the county would hear about the
latest development in the melodrama that the ranch
was becoming. But if they didn't inform the police,
there wouldn't be a record of it, and if something
else happened…

She swallowed back the bile that rose in her throat.

Nothing else would happen. They had gotten the
person responsible for the murders. They might have
had a bad track record, and a bit of a target on their
backs, but that didn't mean the entire world wanted
to take them down. Maybe it *was* just someone's
spare gas.

"Is there oil in it?" she asked, motioning to the
green Heineken bottle.

He glanced down at the bottle and swirled it

around, the green glass looking darker, almost as if the liquid inside had a slight red hue. "Yeah, I think so. Why?"

She smiled and some of her fears dissipated. "You know... Maybe someone was just passing through. Maybe you were right. I mean, if it's a mixed gas—"

"It could be for a chain saw. Maybe they were going out onto the federal lands behind the ranch looking for a Christmas tree or something," Colter said, finishing her sentence. "You are freaking amazing, you know that?"

She smiled and tried not to notice the way her heart sped up when he looked at her like that. She tried to reaffirm that her self-esteem wasn't dependent on his approval, but no matter how hard she tried to convince herself, she couldn't fully accept it as truth. He was so darn cute, and when he smiled, it made some of the sharp edges of her dislike soften. He wasn't as bad as she had assumed. If anything, he had a way of making people relax; and that was just the kind of person she needed in her life. Though he couldn't know that. Nothing could happen between them. Not now, not ever. She needed to stay independent, indifferent.

"I'm not amazing." Even to her, she sounded coy. The last thing she wanted him to think was that she was playing some kind of demure game to get him to fall in love. She wasn't and would never be that kind of woman—a woman who belonged more on the debutante circuit, the kind who could turn on the Southern charm with the simple wave of a hand.

He slipped his hand into hers and she stared at it in shock for a moment before letting go of him and turning away. He couldn't like her. She couldn't like him. If he knew the truth, he would want nothing to do with her.

"Wait. I'm sorry, Whit," he called after her, but she didn't slow down as she made her way back to the office.

She couldn't let herself turn around. She couldn't let him see the look in her eyes that she was sure was there—a look which begged for him to touch her; more, to love her with every part of his soul. She desperately wanted a love like that, but just because she wanted something, that didn't mean that she should have it. Not when she might or might not have been done running.

The dog scrambled out of her shirt and jumped to the floor as soon as she closed the door to her office. The poor thing was covered in dirt and muck, and a piece of what looked like chewed gum was stuck to its ribs. The little thing rushed over to Milo's bed and snuggled into the pile of blankets. She was never going to be able to explain what had happened to the owners if they found out.

If they found out.

She couldn't tell them. No. She chuckled as she thought about all the *Nos* that were suddenly entering her life. Everywhere she turned, every choice she had to make came to that stark end. No.

Things really hadn't changed that much from Kentucky.

When she was home in Louisville, it had been the same. She had told her parents she was leaving, that she was never coming back, that she was following her gut—and every word had been met with the same "No." But they hadn't understood. They had thought it was only out of some selfish need to spread her wings after everything that had happened with Frank. They hadn't known the whole truth, a truth that haunted her every move and threatened to rear its ugly head and reenter her life as long as she stayed there.

And maybe part of it had been the fact that she wanted so much more. She wanted to be around horses again—not close enough to touch, but close. Once you had a love for the animals, there was no turning your back to it, no matter what kind of pain had come from them in the past.

She pressed her back against the office door and closed her eyes. No. She couldn't dig up the past. No.

There was a knock on the door, and it sent vibrations down her spine. She turned around to see Colter standing there, looking at her through the glass.

Why couldn't he get the message that she just wanted him to leave her alone?

Instead of opening the door, she pulled down the shade so he couldn't see her. She couldn't deal with him right now. And seeing him look at her like that, like there was something more than friendship budding between them, it tore at her heart. If something happened…she'd have to run. She'd have to leave this place. She couldn't reveal her past to him or to anyone. She couldn't allow her feelings to make her vulnerable.

"I get it—I have chapped hands," he said with a laugh, and what she assumed was his best attempt at relieving the tension between them, but he was wrong if he thought it would be that easy.

"Or maybe it's not my hands, but you just don't want to talk to me," he continued. "That's fine. I just wanted you to know that everything is back in place and the cattle guard is down. If you need anything just let me know. I'm going to stick around and help my dad." He stood still, almost as if he was waiting for her to answer, but she said nothing.

After a few long seconds, she heard the sounds of his heavy footfalls as he made his way off the porch. She was tempted to peek out from behind the curtain to see where he was going, if he'd finally gotten the message that she wasn't interested, but she stopped herself. She had to be strong.

The phone rang, and she had never been more grateful for the obnoxious sound.

"Dunrovin Ranch Guest Services. This is—"

"We need more towels," a woman said in a shrill voice, cutting her off.

She glanced down at the room number that lit up

the phone's screen. Of course it was Ms. Fancy Pants. She bit the side of her cheek as she thought of all the comebacks she would have liked to say.

"Absolutely, ma'am. I'll have one of our staff bring them to you. Is there anything else you will be needing?"

There was the rumble of a truck and the squeak of brakes from the parking area.

"Where is the nearest club? We wanted to go dancing. You know…honky-tonking, or whatever you rednecks call it."

She swallowed back her anger, only letting a sardonic chuckle slip past. "Ma'am, the only club we have out here is a sandwich. But if you are looking for a bar, we have several. There's the Dog House, which is about five miles from here. It's mostly locals, but on the weekends they usually have a few people dancing." But it was a far cry from the country-style bar that always seemed to fill the movie screens in which everyone was dancing and there was a mechanical bull in the corner. The Dog House was one step away from being somebody's garage. In fact, it would have made sense if that was what the place had once been.

Ms. Fancy Pants sighed so loudly that Whitney wondered if the woman had put her mouth directly on the mouthpiece. "I guess it will have to do. And I won't even bother asking about restaurants. I'd rather go hungry than eat anything this town has to offer."

Whitney's dislike for the woman mounted with each of the woman's passing syllables.

"We'll be right over." She hung up the phone, unable to listen to the woman's prattling for another second.

There wasn't a snowflake's chance in July that she was going to face the woman who'd just called. She dialed the number for the housekeeper, but the phone rang and rang, and she left the girl who was supposed to be working a message about the towels.

She set down the phone and stared at it for a moment. On second thought, maybe she could ask Colter to help. He didn't work for the ranch, but if he was as interested in her as he seemed to be, he might jump at the chance to come to her aid; and it might get him out of her hair for a bit and give her the time she needed to get back to center about him and her feelings.

She sighed, content with her plan, as she opened the door. There was a black Chevy truck parked in the lot, and a tall, thin blonde had her arms draped around Colter's neck. As Whitney watched, the woman threw her head back with a laugh so high and perfect that it bounced around the courtyard until it was finally, thankfully swallowed up by the dark barn.

It was stupid to stand there and watch as the woman flipped her hair and then ran her fingers over the edges of Colter's jacket collar, but she couldn't make sense of what was happening. Sure, the woman was coming on to him. Whitney could understand a woman's attraction to the trim firefighter with a gift when it came to making people at ease, but she couldn't understand the swell of jealousy and unease that filled her as she watched.

He had held her hand, yet now his hands were on the blonde's hips. Was Mr. Eligible Bachelor really Mr. Taken?

Had he been playing her? He had to have been. Heck, he was probably thanking his lucky stars right at that very moment that she had turned him down in time for Ms. Blonde in Tight Jeans to come and wrap her model-ish body around him like a thin blanket.

She gritted her teeth, making them squeak so loudly that it was a wonder he hadn't heard them even at a distance.

The mysterious woman moved to her tiptoes and gave Colter a kiss on the cheek.

It was the last straw.

Whitney turned around and went back inside, slamming the door in her wake. That was fine. If Colter wanted to be with every one of the town's available women, that was fine. He could be with all of them except her. She had better things to do with her time.

On the wall, just beside the door, was a picture of Colter in his bunker gear, a smile on his face. It was ironic. Here was a man who was sent into the flames to save people's lives, but the best thing he had done for her was to save her from falling in love.

Chapter Four

Colter squirmed out of Sarah's grip. At one point he wouldn't have minded having her hands all over him, but not now—not with everything that had happened between them. That attempt at a relationship had crashed harder than the housing market. She cared about only two things: her catering business and how she could make herself happy—no matter the cost to others. Sure, the blonde chef was cute, but beauty was a depreciating asset; being genuine, kind and selfless was far more important than any outward attributes.

He glanced back over his shoulder toward the office where Whitney was working. He could have sworn he'd heard a door slam, yet thankfully, she was nowhere in sight. He would have hated for her to get the wrong idea.

"Colter, when are you going to take me out again?" Sarah asked, running her finger down the buttons on the front of his shirt.

He took hold of her hand and lowered it gently

as he gave her a firm but unwavering smile. "It was fun, but—"

"But what?" she asked, fluttering her eyelashes up at him.

He hated this kind of confrontation. The last thing he wanted to do was hurt her or lead her on, but she was making it difficult.

"But we just don't *fit*. You know what I mean?" he said, trying to take the path of least resistance.

"I bet we could fit together if we just tried, Colter," she said, her voice soft and airy. "I just… You know when we went out, I had just broken up with Kent. I wasn't at my best. I'd like another shot."

"It's not you—"

"It's *me*." She stepped back from him. "Get a new line. Or at least just learn how to tell the woman the truth. If you're not into me, that's fine…" Sarah flipped her hair back off her neck and straightened her jacket like she could simply brush off his rejection.

"Sarah, it really isn't you. I'm just not looking for anything right now." He glanced back to the ranch office as the weight of the lie rolled off his tongue and fell hard. Sarah was right; he wasn't into her. He didn't know why he was bothering to lie other than to save her feelings. The woman he really wanted was Whitney, and she wanted absolutely nothing to do with him.

"When you are looking…I'll be waiting," she said,

her playful smile returning as though she thought there was still room to hope.

He gave a resigned sigh. "Why are you here?"

"I need to finalize the catering details with your mom. Is she around?"

He motioned to the house. "I think she's inside."

"Are you coming to the party?" Sarah asked.

There was no right answer. If he said no, she would see him there and be upset, but he knew if he admitted he was going to be there, she would pressure him for something. He didn't feel like dancing around another come-on.

His father walked out of the house and made a beeline for the barn. "Actually, I need to run along and help my father set things up."

Her face fell with another rejection, but before she could say anything he jogged toward his father.

"I'll see you at the party, then?" she called after him, but he didn't bother to turn around; instead he slipped into the safety of the barn.

Throughout his life this kind of thing seemed to be a recurring theme—the women he didn't want were desperate for him to commit to them, but the women he really wanted to date wouldn't give him the time of day. He dated a lot, but it seemed like things never went too far. With the last woman, he'd gone on one date and she'd spent the entire time talking about her job. They had hit it off all right, they had been able to talk, but, like all the other women he'd gone out with, the woman wasn't what he was looking for. The way things were going, he was never going to have another serious relationship.

Maybe he was just destined to be on his own. To some degree, he liked it that way. His fridge carried only the staples—meat log, cheese and mayonnaise. It was just like the rest of life—simple, uncluttered and what some people might have considered a bit habitual. If he did end up finding himself in a relationship, he'd have to give his routine up—women were never simple. None being more complicated than the curiosity that was Whitney Barstow.

He chuckled as he imagined her walking into his house. She'd probably turn around and walk right out if she saw how bare the place was.

It was just easier this way, deep in his world of habit and minimalism—even if it was a bit lonesome at times. He could deal with lonesome. At least it meant that he wouldn't have to deal with heartbreak.

As the word sank in, the thoughts of his biological father moved to the front of his mind. He had only one memory of the man. Colter was two years old, and his father was leaving him and his brother Waylon on the fire department's doorstep. He had just woken up and his eyes were still grainy from the residue of sleep. Yet he could still see his father's eyes, the color of rye whiskey and their edges reddened with years of what he knew now was hard living. More than his eyes, he could remember the raspy smoke-riddled words he'd last said to them: "Boys," he'd whispered, making sure he didn't give himself away to the firemen just behind the doors. "You all don't go into the flames. When life burns at ya...*run*."

Opening himself up for a relationship was just running into the flames.

"I see Sarah's at it again," his adoptive father, Merle, said as he wrapped a bit of baling twine around his arm.

Colter grabbed a handful of pellets and let the mare at the end of the stalls nibble it out of his hand.

"She's still...Sarah..." He said her name like a verb, and it was met with his father's chuckle.

"Well, at least you can't say that she's a quitter. One of these days she'll get ya tied down. Come hell or high water."

"If she does, I'll be in hell all right." He rubbed the old girl's neck, running his fingers down her silken coat. "What can I help you with?"

"If you're really that afraid of going back out and facing your ex, I could use some help getting down the decorations for the party," his father said, motioning toward the hayloft. "We need the lights and the rest of the wreaths. Your mother is making a fuss about everything being just perfect."

Colter didn't need his father to tell him why or how much was riding on their success.

"Did we sell any more tickets?" he asked as he made his way over to the ladder that led up to the hayloft and stepped up on the bottom rung.

"We're up to about fifty. Some donations are coming in, but as of right now we are thinking that we're only going to just about break even on the thing. We're going to need to sell at least a hundred more tickets."

"Who knows what will happen?" Colter said, making his way up the ladder so his father wouldn't see the concern that undoubtedly filled his features. "Last year we had a lot of people show up at the door, right?"

"That's what we're banking on."

Colter could hear the concern in his father's voice.

"I'd hate to have to start letting people go, but if things don't turn around…"

Whitney hadn't been on the ranch that long. If his parents decided to start laying off staff, he had no doubt that they would do it as fairly and equitably as possible—which meant it would be based on time at the ranch, and Whitney would be among the first to be let go. He couldn't let that happen.

Colter stepped off the ladder as he reached the top and made his way over to the corner where his parents kept the Christmas supplies for the barn. There were green and red tubs, each carefully marked with WREATHS, LIGHTS and TREE DECORATIONS. He loved how meticulous they kept everything. It made life so much easier—when there were labels to everything and instructions on how to keep things from going out of control.

The floor was covered in a thick layer of dust and scattered bits of broken hay. It was warm from the bodies of the horses below and it carried the sweet scent of grass. He remembered coming up here as a kid, hiding in the boxes and making forts with the horses' blankets. He and Rainier, being the two youngest brothers, had spent most of their time up here, close to the horses and the things they loved the most.

He sucked in a long breath as he thought of the careening path to disaster that Rainier's life had taken. If only his parents had made a label, or a set of instructions, for his brother, maybe his life would have gone down a different path.

Colter pulled the top bucket off the stack and moved toward the ladder. "I'll hand this down and grab another."

The floor creaked loudly, and as he took another step, the board beneath his foot shifted. The box in his hands blocked his view, and as he twisted to check his footing, there was a loud crack. The board gave out, and before he could move away, he was falling.

The jagged edges of the wood tore at his legs as he fell through the floor. The pain was raw and surreal, almost as though it was happening to someone else.

He'd always had this fear, but in his mind's eye, he'd always thought that something like this would happen only at his job, when a floor was burning out from underneath him—not in the safety and security of his parents' barn. His world, the one he'd created in his mind where everything was controlled and safe, was betraying him. It was almost the same feeling he'd had as a child… And he couldn't believe he was back here again—feeling powerless as his world collapsed around him.

He threw the bucket and a strange, strangled sound escaped him—the guttural noise as instinct took over. The box clattered onto the floor, the lid flying open and a garland spilling out. Holding out his hands, he scratched at the floor around him. He had to stop. He had to catch himself before he hit the ground below.

His father made a thick sound, somewhere between a gasp and a call to help, just as his fingers connected with the needlelike points of the broken floor. The wood pierced his hands, but he gripped tight. Holding on in an effort to slow his fall.

Though he was strong, his elbows strained with his weight as he jerked to a stop. His feet dangled in the air, just above the bucket of pellets.

There was the grind of metal of the door and the sound of Whitney gasping behind him.

"Colter!" she called, a sharp edge of fear in her voice.

There was the warmth of blood as it slipped down his leg and spilled into the top of his boot. He let go of the wood and fell into the galvanized bucket. It tipped with his weight as it broke his fall, spilling the horses' treats onto the dirt floor.

He threw his arms out, catching himself as he fell, but all it did was slow his descent into the dirt, muck and bits of the broken flooring. For a moment he lay there, taking mental stock of his body. He'd jarred his ankle and he was cut up, but he was going to be fine.

"Colter, are you all right?" Whitney asked, rushing to his side. She touched his shoulder gently, almost as though she would hurt him even more if she pressed too hard.

"Yeah, yeah… I'm fine," he said, trying just as much to convince himself as her. He pushed himself up to sitting. His jeans were torn and there was a deep gash on the side of his leg. The blood was flowing from it, dotted with bits of sawdust and dirt from the ground.

"What in the hell happened?" his father asked.

Colter looked up at the floor. Where he had fallen through, the plywood was jagged on one end, but suspiciously straight on three other sides. He picked up a bit of the flooring that had landed on the ground beside him.

There, on the bit of wood, were the distinctive marks of a saw blade. He lifted the piece for his father and Whitney to see. "Everyone at the ranch knew we would be going up there for the decorations for Yule Night."

His father took the piece of broken lumber and turned it around in his hands, inspecting the marks. "No, Colter… It had to be just some kind of accident. Maybe one of the volunteers just cut through the floor on accident. These things happen."

Colter could hear the lie in his father's voice.

No one would cut almost a perfect rectangle in the

floor by accident. Anyone in their right mind would know the likelihood of someone getting hurt if they stepped on the spot—a spot he'd had to step on in order to get to the boxes. Someone had intended to set a trap—albeit a poor one, one that would hurt anyone who went up there and not someone specific.

He thought of the bottle of oil and gas they had found. While he had tried to convince himself the device wasn't a threat, and was just some random discarded item, now he couldn't be so sure. The odds of two things like this happening on the same day had to be slim to none.

Yet the bottle hadn't been in a place where it would do much damage. In fact, if they hadn't come across it by accident, it could simply have been covered by more snow in the coming days. Unless someone had dropped it there in an attempt to not be seen carrying it. It didn't make sense.

If anything, this all seemed like the ill-conceived plan of a teenager, or else this was someone who wanted to simply send a message—a warning that Dunrovin was coming under attack.

Chapter Five

She could understand acting tough, but Whitney couldn't understand Colter's need to pretend his body wasn't racked by pain. He walked with a limp that he couldn't disguise as they made their way to the ranch house.

"Let me clean you up," she said, motioning to his torn pants and the blood that stained the cloth.

"Don't worry—I'll be fine. It's just a little flesh wound," he said, but the darkness in his eyes and the deep, controlled baritone of his voice gave his pain away.

"Don't be so stubborn. Flesh wound or not, it needs to be cleaned up. And that's to say nothing about maybe going to the emergency room."

Colter shook his head. "There's no way I'm going to the doctor." He lifted the injured leg like it was stiff as he made his way up the stairs and into the house.

She followed him inside and pointed to the oversize leather chair that sat beside the fireplace in the living room. "Sit down. I'll be right back."

His mouth opened as though he considered protesting for a moment, but as he looked at her, he clammed up and hobbled over to the chair and thumped down.

She made her way to the bathroom and got the first-aid kit out of the closet. She was still angry with him. Hurt or not, he'd had his hands all over the blonde in the driveway.

Though she shouldn't have been jealous, she couldn't help it from swelling in her like a fattening tick. She had no claim on Colter Fitzgerald. In fact, no one ever seemed to have a solitary claim on the man. He dated too much and too often for her to let herself even think about him. Yet she couldn't help her thoughts as they drifted to the way he had looked holding the puppy.

No. She couldn't let the thought of how cute he was alter the fact that he usually drove her crazy. They couldn't be a thing. She wasn't looking for a relationship—especially not with a man like him.

She walked down the hallway. As she turned the corner, the blonde and Eloise were standing beside Colter. Before they could see her, she ducked into the tiny little room that was Merle and Eloise's private office. She felt out of place and unwelcome in the room that was neatly organized, its bookshelves color-coordinated with three-ring binders and busi-

ness books. She stood there listening as the blonde
fawned over the hurt Colter.

Whitney stared around the room. She shouldn't
be in here, but there was no way she was going to
walk out in the living room and fake nice with the
woman who was clearly head over heels for Colter—
and, if truth be told, probably more up his alley than
Whitney was.

The lump of jealousy inside her swelled further,
threatening to burst.

She stepped back, bumping against the desk as
she tried to make physical distance work in the place
of the emotional distance she needed. A piece of
paper slipped to the floor, landing with a rustle at
Whitney's foot.

Leaning down, she picked up the page. It was a
bill from Cattleman's Bank to the tune of more than
five thousand dollars. Printed on the top, with large
red letters, was the word *Overdue*. Though it wasn't
her bill, a feeling of sickness passed over her as she
stared at the number at the bottom. There was no
worse feeling than looking at a bill that you knew
couldn't be paid.

She had seen those kinds of things over and over
as a child when her parents were going through their
divorce. The red letters were like shining beacons
from a time in her life that she never wanted to remember, yet was forced to face as she looked at the
paper in her hands.

No wonder everyone on the ranch had seemed on

edge. She had known things were tight with her employers, but she had no clue that things were this bad.

Laying the paper back on the stack of bills in the inbox, she stepped away from the desk and the memories it wrought.

Maybe they weren't as bad off as she was assuming. Maybe it was just one bill that had slipped through the cracks. She was tempted to flip through the other bills that were there, but she stopped herself. It wasn't her business. And even if she knew, there was nothing she could do to change the outcome.

On the other hand, it was her future at stake. If they couldn't pay their regular bills, then there was no possible way that they could continue to carry a staff. She had been lucky to get the job, and it was only when she'd told Eloise about her life in Kentucky that the woman had told her to come to Montana.

The woman had been so kind to her, even offering to pay for her flight here, which now, seeing what she had, Whitney knew the woman and the ranch couldn't afford.

And now she would just have to turn around and go home. She wouldn't be able to find another job in the tiny community that was Mystery, Montana. There was little in the way of anything here, and no one would want to hire a girl like her—one with a past spattered throughout the media.

Whitney stared at the papers. Once again, her future was at the mercy of the world around her, and there was nothing she could do to control her destiny.

She rushed out of the office, unable to stand the indelible red ink at the top of the bill a second longer. The blonde was still standing with Colter, but before Whitney could turn and rush back down the hall, Eloise noticed her.

"There she is," Eloise said, waving her over. "Whitney, have you met Sarah?"

She felt like a dead man walking as she made her way to the living room. Sarah was smiling, her radiant white teeth just as straight and perfect as the rest of her.

"So nice to meet you, Whitney," she said, reaching out to shake her hand.

"Likewise." Whitney played along, but broke away from the handshake as quickly as she could. She didn't want to meet Colter's girlfriend, or friend with benefits, or whatever it was that this girl was to him.

"Sarah is catering the party," Eloise added, almost as though she could sense the tension between the two women.

Whitney forced herself to smile in an attempt to comfort Eloise. Her friend didn't need to worry about some drama that was happening between her and Sarah. Based on the paper she had just seen, there were already enough things going on in Eloise's life.

"That's great. I'm sure it's going to be marvelous," Whitney said, her voice dripping with sugary sweetness put there only for Eloise.

Colter looked up at her and frowned. "Are you okay?" he asked.

"Sure. Just fine," she said, but she looked away out of the knowledge that if he looked at her face he would see just how bad she was at lying. She grabbed the first-aid kit out from under her arm. "Here," she said, handing it to him.

He took the box but looked up at her like he wanted to ask her to help him.

She glanced over at Sarah.

Eloise took Sarah by the arm. "Why don't we run along and finish up going over the menu? You were saying something about the shrimp?"

Sarah opened her mouth to protest being pulled away from the man she was clearly moving in on, but before she could speak Eloise was herding her toward the kitchen.

Whitney walked toward the front door, uncomfortable with being so close and alone with Colter. There were pictures on the wall of the staff over the years, and for a moment she stared up at them.

There was a man in one of the pictures from the early '90s. His hair was slightly longer than everyone else's and his eyes looked dark, almost brooding. As she stared at his features, something about him felt familiar—perhaps it was the look on his face, or the way that he seemed alone when he was surrounded by others, but she couldn't quite put her finger on it.

Colter grumbled and cringed as he limped his way over to her side and looked up at the pictures. "This place has seen a lot of things."

"And a lot of people come and go," she said, instinctively glancing toward the office and then toward the kitchen, where she could hear the garbled sound of Eloise and Sarah talking.

He glanced toward the kitchen.

"What is going on between you two?" she asked, motioning toward the closed kitchen door.

His eyes widened and his mouth gaped like he was waiting for the right answers to simply start falling out.

"I saw you guys in the parking lot." She turned away from him, unable to look him in the face as she talked. "I know it's not any of my business. But I know…I know you date a lot. And I don't want her to think…"

"She can think whatever she wants," he said, finally finding his voice.

"So you're not dating?"

He shifted his weight, but jerked as though the movement caused him pain. "I… She and I, we were a thing once. It wasn't anything serious."

"But she's your ex."

He looked over at her, catching her gaze. "I would hardly call what she and I had a relationship, so I wouldn't really call her an ex."

"I would," she said, feeling the acidic tone of her words straight to her bones.

He stared at her for a moment before looking away, and her heart sank. She shouldn't have come at him like that. They all had a past, and if he looked too deeply into hers, she had no doubt that he would find things that he didn't like, as well. Her thoughts moved to the fire and the man who had caused it.

Colter turned to walk away, but she stopped him as she grabbed his wrist.

"I'm sorry," she said as he turned to look at her. "I'm just upset. You didn't do anything wrong. And I have no reason to be jealous. You can date whoever you want."

It wasn't as if Colter liked her anyway. If he got to know her, everything would fall apart and whatever crush he had on her would rapidly diminish.

"I don't want to date just anyone. The only one I'd love to take out is you," he said, pulling her hand off his wrist and wrapping her fingers between his. "From the moment you came here, it's all I wanted."

She wanted to give in to the joy of hearing those words, but her reality wouldn't allow it. She was so close to losing her job, her place here, and that was to say nothing about the odd things that were starting to happen around the place.

She pulled her hand from his. "I don't know who you think I am, but I'm telling you that I'm not perfect. I'm not the kind of woman who most men want to date. If you just got to know me a little more, you would see that you wouldn't want a woman like me."

"I know you, whether you want to admit it or not."

She gave a sardonic chuckle. "Just because we've been passing each other on the ranch since I got here, that doesn't mean you know me. You have merely seen me. There are things in my past that a man like you would never accept. We have fundamental differences. Number one—that you have more dates than a fruitcake. I don't want a man whose attention I have to struggle to keep."

"Unless we go out, how do you know if we have fundamental differences?" He leaned against the chair closest to him. "And wait… Does fruitcake even have dates in it?"

She groaned as she tried not to smile. He might have been right, she didn't know if there were dates in fruitcake, but she was never going to admit it. He never ceased to irritate her. He couldn't take anything seriously—but then again, it was one of the things she couldn't help being attracted to.

"Just sit down," she said, pointing to the chair he leaned on. "I will fix your leg. As long as you promise not to ask me out again."

"Today or ever?" he said, giving her a cheeky grin.

She sighed, not wanting to give him the answer she should have. She equally loved and hated the feelings he created within her. It was so much easier to not give in to her attraction, to keep out of the reach of any man's attentions. As soon as men entered her life, only bad things seemed to follow in their wake—drama, intrigue and danger.

Love was just too risky—especially with a man like Colter, the most eligible bachelor in the county.

He plopped down into the chair and she went to get the first-aid kit. He pulled up his shredded pants leg, unveiling his bloodied and badly cut leg. Slivers of wood were embedded in his skin.

"Maybe you should go into the emergency room?" she asked, sitting down on the floor at his feet.

He waved her off. "It's fine as long as we get it cleaned out."

It struck her how strong he was. He had to be hurting, yet he still fought through it to make jokes with her. She didn't want to admit it, but he really was an incredible man. Not that she was in the market for a man—no matter how incredible.

"You didn't give me an answer about asking you out again," he said as she set about cleaning the wound on his leg.

She patted at the cut with the gauze soaked in hydrogen peroxide as she tried to come up with the right answer. "It's not you… You're great. It's just that right now…" She glanced toward the office.

His face dropped and she watched as the hope faded from his eyes. It was almost as if part of his soul had seeped from him, and she hated herself for making something like that happen. Yet she couldn't change her mind. She had to stick to her guns.

"Besides," she continued, "you need to focus on where you're walking. If you think about me all the time— I mean, look at what happened this time." She motioned to his leg. "You fell through a floor. I'm a risk to your health." As the words escaped her, she couldn't help thinking about how many times that had been true for the people she had gotten close to, throughout her life.

No matter where she went, or what she did, she only brought danger, sadness and loss to the ones she loved. To protect him, and the people of the ranch, she could never love again.

Chapter Six

Overnight the sky had opened and fresh glittering snowflakes adorned Colter's front yard. The weatherman was calling for another six inches of snow today and possibly another six tomorrow. Yet in rural Montana, six inches could turn out to be two inches, or it could be two feet—it all depended on the way the wind decided to blow and the fickle whims of the winter storm.

He loved this time of year. Some hated the cold and the constant grayness that came with living in the valley, but he'd always thought of the world around him like a blanket. The mountains were his borders and the clouds were his cover, as though he were protected from the brutal world thanks to the bosom of the world itself.

He pulled on a red sweater his mother had given him last Christmas. He needed to get back to the ranch. His parents would need his help plowing and getting ready. There were only two more days until the party. He'd need to fix the floor of the barn. Not to mention being on hand to greet the visitors who would be starting to arrive for the ranch's holiday festivities.

If truth be told, though his parents would appreciate his help, he knew they could do it on their own—what and who he really wanted to help was Whitney and the poor little dog they had saved. Or, if she asked, that would be a convenient excuse for finding his way to the ranch's main office.

The snow crunched under his boots as he walked out to his pickup. He started it, letting the engine warm up and stave off the bitter cold. His breath was a white cloud even in the cab of the truck. According to the dashboard temperature gauge, it was ten below. This kind of weather only lent itself to three things—breakdowns, house fires and frostbite.

He wouldn't be surprised if he got called into work. It would be an overtime shift, but the last thing he wanted to do right now was find himself there. His hand and leg were sore from yesterday's fall. He'd be all right, but it would be an annoyance that he would have to ignore in order to do his job—and anytime something like this happened, he always had a sinking fear that it could hinder his attempt to save someone's life. He hated the thought of letting someone else down thanks to his own weakness.

As he drove toward the ranch, his mind wandered to his other weakness—Whitney. He couldn't get her out of his thoughts. She didn't want to be with him; she had made that clear. Yet, when he was around her, there was just some…a spark. Something seemed to buzz between them, and from the look in her eyes, she couldn't ignore the feeling, either.

He just had to be around her, even if it wasn't as anything more than a friend. He was simply drawn to her. Maybe it would turn into something more than it was, and maybe it wouldn't, but at the very least he could have her in his life.

Whitney really was one of the most confusing women he'd ever met. One minute she seemed open to the world and a future, and the next it was like a curtain fell over her and she slipped back into the shadows of her thoughts and closed him out. Colter understood it. He had seen the look a thousand times with his brother Waylon. It was the look that came with loss and pain.

She had never really talked about her life, but she didn't need to tell him in order for him to understand that she had some baggage. Everyone had a past. Though he tried hard to hide from his, enveloping it with humor and lightheartedness, it didn't hurt any less when he pressed too hard against it. If she would only talk to him, maybe they could work through it together.

He hoped.

Or maybe her secrets were darker than he could ever imagine. Maybe she'd killed a man. Left someone on the side of a road. He laughed at his ridiculous thought. She wasn't the kind. She was a tad rough around the edges, but was soft in all the ways that were important. Yet, as much as he was attracted to her, he couldn't help feeling like he was in the dark. She was hiding something from him, something she feared sharing with anyone, something that he desperately wanted to know.

Maybe that was what he was most attracted to her for—her mysteriousness. She challenged him in a way no other woman had. She was like a quest, and it made him want her that much more.

As he neared the ranch, there was a line of cars in the middle of the road. One of the drivers was standing beside his car, holding up his cell phone as though he was searching for a signal.

Colter stopped next to the man and rolled down his window. "What's going on?"

"The road's blocked. And of course there isn't a cell phone signal to be had," the man said, his voice flecked with a Northeastern accent, as he pushed his phone deep into his pocket. "And I don't even know if we're in the right place." He motioned to his car.

It was a white rental, the kind that most picked up when they arrived at their little airport. It had regular tires that made a day like this, one in which everything was slick and treacherous, that much more dangerous.

"You heading to Dunrovin?" Colter asked.

The man nodded. "We heard that it was magical, but so far all we're finding is crappy roads and poor technology. Even your airport was like walking into a living room from the seventies."

Colter couldn't help the laugh that escaped him. If he had to explain to someone what the place looked like, he wouldn't have come up with something as perfect as the man's description. The airport was all orange and brown, and its walls were accented with the dark cherrywood that harked back to the day it had been built.

"No offense," the man added, his breath clouding the air.

"None taken. Admittedly there are times when even I have to agree we are a little bit behind the rest of the country."

"But that's all part of its charm," the man said. "Except when you need to make a call." He laughed.

"Don't worry about it. I got a phone that works. Why don't you just go and get warmed up? I'll make sure you get to the ranch."

The man gave him an appreciative nod and, tucking his face into the collar of his jacket, jogged back to his car.

Colter got out of his truck and made his way to the front of the line. There, in the world of white, was a fallen pine. Its dark green boughs and its buckskin trunk were partly masked in newly fallen snow. Yet, as he neared the tree that lay across the road, he could see the fresh cut marks of a chain saw at the tree's base.

Tacked to the center of the tree, between some branches, was a red envelope. It was flecked with snow and he blew it off, his breath warming some of the flakes enough to make fat wet blobs on the paper that looked almost like tears.

He grabbed it and opened the seal. The cold winter chill bit at his fingers as he pulled the card from the envelope. The card had a picture of his family and the staff in front of the ranch's sign. He recognized it as the family's yearly newsletter. They sent it out to everyone in the community and former guests. Thousands had to have gone out. Yet this one was different. Each of the people's faces had been x-ed out with a black marker. He flipped over the card. On the back it read:

Mess with my family. I'll mess with yours.
This is WAR.

Chills rippled down his spine as he looked at the jagged handwriting.

The bomb, the floor…it all made sense. Someone had been trying to send them a message. Someone was coming after them.

He stared at the letter. Whose family had they been messing with?

His thoughts moved to William Poe and his wife's death. William had threatened them, as he had sworn that their family was to blame for his wife's demise, but he wouldn't do something so treacherous. He was the kind who would pull political strings, not obstruct roads to deter guests from making it to the ranch, or send makeshift Molotov cocktails as a warning.

His wife's killer's only relatives had been Christina and her young daughter, Winnie, who were both in Fort Bragg with Waylon until they came back in a few weeks to celebrate Christmas. Truth be told, Colter had a feeling that part of the reason Christina had been so willing to go with Waylon was that it was so hard to face the community after everything that had happened with her sister.

If only his answers were so easy. Right now all he had was a threatening note, the remnants of a bomb and a series of scrapes and bruises.

He glanced back at the note, trying his best to see something about it that would help him get an idea, yet he found himself concentrating on the dark ink of the letters.

Maybe there was something going on, something deeper in the past that he didn't know about. His parents didn't share everything.

He walked back to the guy in the car and tapped on his window as he stuffed the envelope into his pocket.

"Is there anything you can do?" the guy asked.

Colter barely heard the man as he ran his fingers over the edge of the envelope in his pocket. "Huh?"

"The tree," the guy said, frowning. "Is there something you can do?"

"Oh, yeah. No worries. I have a chain saw in the back of my truck."

"You carry a saw around with you?" the guy asked, giving him a look of disbelief.

In Montana, there was a culture of live and let live, and with that came a certain amount of self-reliance. If you needed something fixed, or to get yourself out of a jam, it was up to you and your ingenuity. In his world, he had to be like a Boy Scout and always be prepared.

"This is hardly my first tree across a road. It ain't nothing," he said, forcing a smile. "I'll get it out of the way in a sec."

It took a few minutes thanks to the pain in his calf, but before long he'd cut the tree into manageable pieces and loaded it all into the back of his truck for next year's firewood. He waved the cars on, but all he could think about as he worked was the fact that someone had done all this to send them a message.

If he hadn't come along, the guests would have been stuck out there for hours until someone found out about the tree. It would have been an even worse start to what, for many of their guests, was meant to be a restful vacation away from these kinds of headaches.

The ranch was bustling as he arrived. The man he'd talked to had a key in his hand and was making his way to his room as Colter parked. Luckily, the guy had a smile on his face. He must have been talking to Whitney. She always had a way of making people happy. It was why she was so good at her job, and no doubt why his mother had hired her—even though it had to be hard on the ranch's finances.

Another couple walked out of the office. They were carrying hot chocolates, complete with big white marshmallows and cups that looked like snowmen.

He waited a moment for the guests to make it to the ranch's assortment of houses and to their appointed rooms. It felt good as he watched the movement of the comings and goings of the place. It reminded him of the many good years that they'd had, years when there were so many guests that they would be booked six months to a year in advance.

They would get there again. He knew it.

He reached into his back pocket, took the envelope out and glanced at the card. Someone wanted this all to end just as much as he wanted it all to continue. The perpetrator was right—the place was at war. He'd have to give this place everything he could to bring it back to life—and a bright future—even if that meant giving up his own dreams.

He put the envelope on his dashboard and sat back for a moment. What were his dreams?

It had been a while since he'd really given any thought to his own life and where he wanted to go. As it was, his job was the kind that had a certain cap. He'd never get rich doing what he was doing. He'd probably never become the fire marshal or the captain, no matter how many years he put into the place—the odds were stacked against him for that kind of job. However, none of that really mattered to him.

If he had to put words to his true feelings and desires, what he wanted most was a family of his own. He thought about Waylon and his daughter, Winnie. He loved that girl, and it made his heart heavy to think of her all the way across the country. She had brought such joy and lightheartedness to the ranch.

He was ready to have a life that revolved around the smile and cheers of a kid like her. In fact, it would be great to have children about the same ages as his brothers'. It would bring them all back together again, all back to this wondrous place and to share his world with.

More than that, he wanted a woman in his life, a wife whom he could share it all with—the joy of having a family, spending nights around a warm fire and taking the horses out for a ride on the weekends. He wanted a wife who would light up when she saw him come home. He wanted a wife to help him make a home, a wife who could be his partner in everything life brought.

Until now, he hadn't realized how lonely he was. Sure, he had his parents and brothers, but it wasn't the same as being in a loving and committed relationship—a connection that was true and deep. He longed for the kind of bond in which they could finish each other's sentences, become their better selves.

He wanted to be completed.

Whitney walked out of the office and, not seeing

him, made her way toward the end of the house. She picked up from the ground an orange plastic box that held his father's chain saw and made her way to the woodshed. He reached down and was about to open the truck's door, but stopped. Why would she have had his father's chain saw? It didn't make sense.

He sat back and watched her as she disappeared into the woodshed. A few minutes later she came out and tucked her hair behind her ear and locked the door.

She reached down and picked a bit of sawdust from her jacket and flicked it into the snow and glanced around like she was checking to make sure no one had seen her. Was it possible that she had been putting the saw away after she had used it to fell the tree in the road?

He shook the thought from his head. Just because he didn't know who had sent the threatening note didn't mean everyone around him was guilty. And the last person he could see being responsible for the fallen tree was her. She had no reason to disrupt the flow of guests. Her future was just as dependent on the success or failure of the ranch as the rest of them. It would have been counterintuitive.

Yet whoever was behind the sabotage that was occurring had to know a bit about the comings and goings of the ranch.

He moved slightly and Whitney caught sight of him and waved. He smiled and returned her wave before getting out of his truck.

"What are you doing out here?" she asked, approaching him and stopping by the front steps of the porch leading to the office.

He couldn't ignore the way she quickly glanced back over her shoulder toward the shed.

Her eyes were bright and her face was red from the cold, but she stood there and waited until he walked to her side. "I thought I'd come out and give you all a hand after the storm. Thought you'd need a little plowing to be done or something."

"That was thoughtful of you," she said. "How's your leg doing?"

He lifted it up high for her, wiggling it about. "It's still attached. I'm sure it will be fine. Just a few scrapes and bruises."

"If you want, I can take another look at it for you."

Though it was bitterly cold, a warmth rose to his cheeks as he thought about her hands traveling all over his leg once again. It had been a long time since he'd let a woman touch him. Sure, she hadn't meant it like that, but there had been something about it. And she hadn't made it a secret that she had hated him being around Sarah.

She had seemed so upset, jealous almost, at the thought of him having once been with Sarah. And as badly as he wanted to ask her if she was okay now, the last thing he wanted to bring up was her feelings from last night. Especially when she had made him promise not to ask her out again.

He'd never been the desperate kind. He had enough

self-respect to know when a woman didn't want him in her life, but he couldn't ignore the spark between them and how he still felt the same charge now that she was near. Sure, she had rebuffed his advance and he wasn't about to make another pass at her, but that didn't mean he didn't hope she would come around.

She started to walk toward the office, and as he stepped after her, he looked back at his truck. There, glaring in the windshield, was the red envelope.

He'd have to call Wyatt and let him know about the letter. But if he was even a tiny bit right that Whitney was involved with this…she would be in trouble. Wyatt could be intense when it came to defending his family. He would make sure, regardless of Colter's feelings toward Whitney, that she—or anyone else responsible—would be sent a message that the Fitzgeralds and Dunrovin weren't to be messed with.

Colter was positive that he had it all wrong. He had just seen something out of context, but until he knew for sure, he couldn't take the risk.

Chapter Seven

Colter was staring at her so intently that it made the hair on the back of her neck rise. He didn't look upset or sad. Instead he was looking at her like she had done some unspeakable thing.

Was this about last night?

She had spent all night tossing and turning as she had gone over every word that she had said to him. By 3:00 a.m. she had finally convinced herself that she had said what needed to be said, albeit she could have been more eloquent. Yet now, standing here with him looking at her like that, she was back to square one in thinking she had gotten things between them all wrong.

"I…I'm sorry about last night," she said, finally breaking the awkward silence between them.

He blinked for a moment, almost as if he were pulling himself back to reality, and his familiar grin returned. The simple action and change made some of the tightness in her chest loosen.

"You're fine. I mean…" He ran his hand over the

fine layer of stubble on the side of his jaw. "I hear you. I don't want you to think that…you know…I won't respect your boundaries. If you don't want to go out with me, I get that. You have nothing to be sorry about."

She had plenty to be sorry about—number one, that he'd actually believed her. She wished she could tell him that it wasn't about him. But there was no going back and fixing what she had broken between them. She could see it in his eyes—he didn't trust her anymore.

Two people couldn't have anything if they didn't have trust.

She wasn't sure what to say that would make the look in his eyes disappear. "Thanks."

"What were you doing?" he asked, glancing toward the woodshed.

"Huh?"

"I saw you with the chain saw. Did you become a lumberjack overnight?" he asked with a chuckle, but the sound was forced and high.

"One of the guests mentioned that it was sitting out when they checked in," she said.

He nodded, but as hard as she tried, she couldn't catch his gaze. "Did they say who put it there?"

In truth, she hadn't even given the saw a real thought. The man in the white car, David Hellman, had just told her about it when he checked in. He'd also told her about a downed tree.

"You don't think I had anything to do with the

thing out in the road, do you?" she asked, taken aback at the sudden realization of what he must have been thinking of her. "I would never do anything to jeopardize this place. Dunrovin is my home. And, if I have my way, I plan to stay here for years to come," she said, not waiting for him to answer her question.

"Years to come?" he asked, his grin widened and some of the seriousness melted away from his gaze.

"I know we don't know each other well," she said, trying to control her temper as she thought about how affronted she was that he would think her low enough to do something to upset the ranch. "But you should know that I'm not the kind of person who would hurt those that I care—"

"About?" he asked, but from his tone she knew what he was really asking was if she cared about him.

Yet all she could think about was that day in the barn, the day of the fire. What she was trying to convince him of was entirely true. She had been the reason her horse had been hurt. She had tried to save him, but if only she'd tried a little harder. And now here she was, with a firefighter again.

"I just mean—" She was cut off by the ranch office's door swinging open.

The little rat dog came loping out, yipping loudly as Eloise followed at its heels. "Where you going?" Whitney asked, motioning toward the little dog.

Milo plodded out of the office. The old ranch dog was a mutt but looked a bit like a Labrador retriever with a shaggy coat. Next to the well-kept Chihuahua, who was complete with a set of red nail polish, he looked even more derelict than he ever had before.

Whitney smiled as Milo stopped beside the little dog and gave it a wet, sloppy kiss on the top of its head, promptly putting a stop to the menace's barking.

"Don't you think she's a little bit out of your league, buddy?" Colter reached down and patted Milo on the head.

The dog looked over at her with his big brown eyes, and she swore that she saw him smile. It was almost as if the dog thought the same thing about her and Colter and was trying to send her some kind of message. She stuck her tongue out at the dog. She didn't need anyone or anything, especially not her closest buddy, trying to remind her of who she was.

Eloise chuckled and turned back to her. "If you wouldn't mind, when you're running into town, I have a note for Sarah about the menu. Would you drop it off? I can't seem to reach her on her cell phone. It's going straight to voice mail and I don't want her to miss a chance to get to the grocery store before they close for the night." Not waiting for an answer, Eloise handed her the note.

She looked down at it and saw Sarah's name printed across it.

Thankfully, Colter reached over and took the note from her hand. "Did you try to text her, Mom?"

Eloise put her hands on her hips and gave her son a matronly glare. "Do you think that I'm really that behind the times?"

Colter shrugged, his smile shining bright. "Okay…"

"Thank you. And when you get the food for… the little dog," she said, like she couldn't remember the dog's name, either, "her owners wanted to remind you that she only eats organic and GMO-free dog food."

Whitney smirked. It hadn't been an hour since she had seen the dog go out with Milo into the pasture. Whatever it ate out there couldn't have been the prized dog food that the owners had requested, but she would make sure to keep that out of her report when and if they called to check on their dog over the next few days.

"No problem. Did they want the filet mignon or the prime rib flavor?" she added with a sarcastic laugh. "But hey, I get it…wanting to give your animals the best." Whitney glanced toward the barn and the stables where a few of the horses had stuck their heads over the gates to watch.

She knew all too well how much she had been willing to sacrifice for the animals she loved.

"If you're running into town, do you mind if I ride along?" Colter asked. "Actually, why don't we take the truck? I need to get some lumber to fix the hole in the hayloft's floor. Unless Dad already did it?" he asked, looking to Eloise.

She shook her head. "Your father's been running around like a chicken with his head cut off all morning. He's out feeding the animals, but I know he was talking about getting the rest of the barn cleaned up before the dance."

"If you see him, tell him not to worry about the floor. I'll take care of it," Colter said, motioning in the direction of the barn. "And when we get back, I'll help him with the rest of it."

Eloise looked over at her and gave her a knowing smile. It was so warm and full of implied meaning that Whitney forced herself to look away, unsure of how to respond. She wished she could just tell Eloise everything, but there were so many things…things she would never understand, and even on the off chance that she did, she could probably never look at Whitney the same way again.

It was just easier this way, keeping an emotional distance from everyone around her. Yet no one at the ranch seemed to understand.

THEY DROVE DOWN Main Street and toward the hardware store. The antiques shop that had once belonged to William Poe's wife was boarded up, but the front windows were still filled with the knickknacks that she had put up for sale before her death. In most places, life had a way of moving on after someone's death, but here in Mystery, it was as if even one person's death was reason for the entire town to go into mourning.

Even though it was getting near Christmas, business was slow in the downtown stores. A few people were carrying shopping bags as they walked out from the drugstore, and one woman had rolls of wrapping paper tucked under her arm.

Colter pulled into a parking spot and turned off the engine. The ride to town had been quiet, almost too quiet. Yet all he could think about was the glaring red envelope on his dashboard and all the things it could mean.

He believed Whitney was innocent—she couldn't have had anything to do with the felled tree—but she hadn't seemed surprised at all when he brought it up. She'd appeared upset only when he broached the subject of her somehow being involved.

From his police buddies he'd learned that when someone was truly innocent they got angry when accused of a crime, and those who were guilty typically gave reasons they wouldn't have done such a thing. She had done both.

He stepped out of the truck and walked around to her side and opened her door. She turned and looked up at him. Her eyes were full of pity and something else that he couldn't put his finger on.

He was making something out of nothing. Being cynical wasn't his strength. He had always left that to Waylon—and now, pressed to be that way, he didn't like it. He liked living in a world where people were innocent until they were proved guilty.

As she stepped out of the truck, he yearned to take her by the hand and help her.

She walked to the sidewalk and turned to face him. "Colter, do you ever think that some things are too big to let go? That no matter how hard you try they will mess up your life forever?"

The question made him stop in his tracks. "Where did that come from?"

She shook her head. "I don't know. I guess I was just thinking about…everything."

He wasn't sure exactly what she meant by that, and if she was talking about them or not, but he wasn't sure he wanted to ask. She was finally opening up to him, and this was one gift that he didn't want to screw up.

"I think everyone has things that happen in their life that they're not proud of. No one is a saint. Life can be messy, but that doesn't mean that we wall ourselves off and stop living."

"Protecting yourself from getting hurt again isn't stopping from living. It's being smart."

To a certain degree he could agree with her. It was so much easier to just not put himself out there— even with her. Rejection could be so hard to deal with. It made people jaded if they let it go too deep.

"I don't want to grow older and be one of those bitter people you see… You know what I mean?" he asked, the question as non-accusatory as possible.

"Are you saying I'm bitter?"

"No… Not at all." He tried to mentally backpedal. "I just mean that I don't want to be unhappy when I get older. When I find the woman I want to marry, I want to be with her forever. I want a life where there is nothing but great happiness—no matter what it takes."

"Life isn't all sunshine and daisies. It's pain and reflection. It's making ends meet when there isn't enough. It's about struggle and hardship. And marriage would be just as hard."

"If you love someone with all your heart, you can get through anything—especially the hard times."

She smiled, but there was a deep pain in her eyes that the smile couldn't camouflage. "Two people can't love each other like that."

He couldn't disagree with her more, and it hurt him to imagine what she had been through in life that could have made her this skeptical and dismissive of what was one of life's greatest pleasures.

"If you don't think so, then you've never really been in love," he said.

Her eyes widened with surprise and she opened her mouth to speak, but held back.

"If you really, truly love someone and they love you back, you can take on the world and whatever it has to throw at you."

"How many times have you been in love?" she asked.

There was nothing quite like walking into an unwinnable situation like that. There was no right answer. "How many times have you?"

She held her hands tightly in front of her and stared down at her fingers. "Just once. And that was enough to show me that maybe love isn't right for me."

"When did it end?"

She sucked in a long breath. "The moment he struck the match."

Chapter Eight

The old adage of still waters running deep crossed his mind, but even that didn't seem to quite fit the woman he wanted to pull into his arms. She was deeper and far more full of secrets than he ever could have guessed, and she was finally deciding to let him into her life and her past. He was honored but at the same time absolutely terrified with the pressure that he could let her down.

"Was he trying to kill you?" he asked. His voice was thick and he tried to swallow back the bile that rose in his throat as he thought about someone coming to hurt her.

"My death wasn't enough for him. He wanted to take away all the things I loved first. He wanted to break me."

"What happened?" He leaned back against the front grille of the truck, relaxing his body in hopes that she would see that he wanted and was ready to listen to whatever she wanted to tell him.

She bit at the skin of her bottom lip. "I don't want to talk about it."

He stood back up, convinced his attempt at subconsciously swaying her to open up thanks to his body language hadn't worked. As he stood, she moved closer to him, so close that he could smell the floral bouquet scent wafting up from her hair. She smelled so good, like freshly washed hair and dryer sheets.

She balled her fists and then opened up her fingers and slipped them into his. "Thanks for just listening. I just needed… I guess I *need* a friend."

"I'm here," he said, lacing his fingers between hers, "for whatever you need."

He hated the dreaded friend-zone, but he would take what he could get from this incredible woman. She had so much to offer the world, if only she would come out of her shell a little bit more—and if he could be the catalyst she needed to feel safe, wanted, and loved again, he'd be more than happy to help.

She squeezed his hand in hers and smiled up at him. "You don't know how much that means to me. I haven't…I haven't talked about what happened ever since I left Kentucky."

"Does my mother know?"

Whitney shook her head. "Only the basics. She knows there was a fire, and I couldn't stay there."

"My mom has always had a big heart. She's probably the only reason that me and my brothers are doing as well as we are."

Whitney went rigid as he ran his thumb over the back of her hand, but as he stroked she started to soften under his touch, just like a horse.

"You know, you and your mom are a lot alike," she said. "You both try to make everyone else around you happy. You're so giving."

It made him happier than she could possibly know that she thought that much of him. Most women only complimented him on his looks or his jeans or some other superficial thing... Not that he minded that they thought him sexy—it was just nice to be recognized as something more.

He lifted her hand, wanting to kiss her skin, but he stopped himself. She only wanted a friend, albeit friends who apparently held hands, but it was up to her to decide the speed of whatever was going on between them. "Thanks," he said, lowering their hands back down. "But really, I'm just as flawed as any other man. I have my quirks."

She smiled and the darkness that had always seemed to fill the space around her lightened. "And those quirks would be...? You know, for research and friendship purposes only."

The way she spoke made a dash of hope move through him. Maybe she did want something more, or maybe he was just a fool for hoping.

"Are you the kind who moves too fast?" she continued, not waiting for him to answer. "Wait...are you a mouth breather?"

"What?" He laughed. "Definitely not a mouth breather. Would that be a deal breaker for you?"

Her smile widened. "I wouldn't date a man who was unkind to his mother. I think that, with some exceptions, a man can be judged by his relationship with his mom."

"Do I pass that test?"

Her eyebrow quirked. "What if I said no?"

The way she teased made the little bit of hope inside him grow.

"If you said no, then I suppose that I would have to hang out with you some more—I would show you what kind of man I really am."

"Hmm… I was going to say that your relationship with your mother was good, but now I'm rethinking it. So much so that we may need to spend a little more time together."

He laughed. "Before I commit to something so extreme, are there any more quirks that I need to know about? You know, major turnoffs?"

She started to lead him toward the hardware store. She looked back at him with a smile, but had started to nibble her bottom lip. He'd noticed the little tic before, and he loved the way it made her lips grow redder—it was almost the same color as if she had just been kissed. And a kiss, just one single kiss, was the only thing in the world he wanted right now.

"Let's see…" she said as they walked into the store. The place smelled like old popcorn and motor oil. "I don't like when a man thinks he can boss me around. And I need someone who's patient."

He had patience in spades and he'd learned not to try to tell a woman what to do a long time ago. He couldn't understand the women who let their lives be controlled by the men they said they loved, and on the flip side, he didn't want or expect to be controlled, either. "The only relationships that I have found to work in my life are when we work in tandem, side by side, and raise each other up. By telling those who we care about what to do... Well, I think it's kind of patronizing. You know what I mean?"

"Yeah, it's almost like you can't think for yourself." She let go of his hand and motioned toward the lumber department. "If you wanted to run and get what you need, I'll get us some popcorn. Sound good?"

She was running from their talk, but he couldn't blame her. As much as he loved talking to her and learning about what made her tick, it was always uncomfortable and challenging to open up and reveal yourself to another person. She might not have realized it, but he held the same fears. It came with who he was, a part of him that was as deeply ingrained as his will to breathe.

He grabbed a cart for the board and moved through the aisle, making quick work of getting the plywood. He pushed the monstrous, wobbling cart through to the front of the store as Whitney came walking toward him. She smiled and lifted up the popcorn like a peace offering. Yet, as she looked at him, she mustn't have noticed the display of Christmas ornaments that were in the middle of the aisle and her foot connected with the corner of the boxes, sending the popcorn in her hands flying. The kernels flew through the air, and as she moved to instinctively correct herself, she fell forward, landing on the floor in a sea of yellow corn.

She glanced up, her mouth opened in shock, and looked toward him to see if he had been watching. He let go of his cart and rushed to her side. She put her forehead down on the concrete floor as he neared.

"Are you hurt?" he asked, kneeling down beside her. "That was a hard fall."

"Ugh," she said, the noise coming from somewhere deep within her. "I can't believe I just did that…and you saw." She started to giggle and she pushed herself up to her knees. "I swear I'm not the klutzy type—I'm no Bella Swan. Really."

"Bella Swan?" he asked, totally confused.

"You know… The girl from *Twilight*."

He laughed. "So you're a fan of vampire novels?" He took her by the arm and helped her to stand. He brushed the front of her jacket off, careful to avoid the gentle curves where her breasts pressed against the firm cloth of her coat.

"I always love a good story," she said, but he noticed that her already red cheeks grew a shade darker.

"Taking out a thousand ornaments at a hardware store is a good one…" He laughed, motioning to the boxes of ornaments that had tumbled on the far side of the stack.

She ran her hands over her face.

He walked around to the other side and started to pick up the boxes and set them up on the remaining stack.

"Are any of them broken?" she asked, moving to his side and picking up a box, flipping it around in her hand.

He looked at the boxes in his hands. "None so far. But hey, if the first ornament that we have to buy together is a broken one, I'll take it."

She stopped moving and stared at him for a moment, making him wish that he hadn't pressed her about anything involving what might or might not have been his hopes of a relationship.

Glancing away, she set the box in her hand on the top of the stack. "If, and only if, we had a relationship, I would hope we would start it without broken things."

The hope inside him grew one size larger, making him think of the Grinch and the little box exploding as his heart grew three sizes. "If we started dating… What would be your ideal first date?"

She kept moving, but he could see her chewing at her lip. "I don't know. What about you?"

He shrugged, picking up another box. "I guess I would want to go horseback riding. It's something I always did as a kid. It always calmed me down when I was having a hard day."

"If someone didn't ride, would that be a deal breaker for you?"

He nodded. "It would be hard. It's a big part of my life. I grew up around horses, you know. They are like other members of the family to me. You know what I mean?"

Her shoulders fell and she turned her back to him. She stopped moving and he could see her shoulders start to quiver. Reaching over, he touched her shoulder and turned her around. A tear slipped down her cheek.

"Are you okay? Did you hurt something when you fell?" he asked, trying to make sense of her spontaneous crying.

"I…I don't ride anymore. I can't." She wiped the tear from her face, the motion so hard that it left a red mark behind. "We…can't… There are so many reasons."

The last thing he had wanted to do was upset her. The hope in him receded. He couldn't fix her. He couldn't make her feel something that she didn't want, or wasn't ready, to feel.

"You don't need to worry about that," he said, but the disappointment rattled through him. "Did you ever ride?"

He scooped the popcorn into a pile and left it beside the stack of ornaments. He was so attracted to her, and all of her perfect imperfections, but she had rejected him.

He had been stupid to hope for anything more than

being her friend. He gave a resigned sigh. He needed to be happy with that, and he would just have to keep reminding himself that it was better to have her as that than nothing at all. At least this way, he could keep her in his life.

She picked up the last ornament. "I used to have the best horse. He was from the Secretariat bloodline. He was worth so much money and I had plans to start using him to stud. His papered name was Runs Like the Wind, but I just called him Rudy."

"What happened?" As soon as he asked, he chastised himself for asking her something so personal. When would he learn that she would balk if he pressed too hard?

Sucking in a long breath, she slowly made her way over to his cart.

The look in her eyes reminded him of a skittish horse—one that had been hurt in the past so badly that it would take a long time for it to be able to trust again. "You don't have to tell me if you don't want to," he continued, trying to make her feel at ease.

"He was… He died in the fire."

"The fire your ex set?"

She glanced around the store, but he couldn't tell if she was looking for her ex or an exit. "He… I tried to save him."

She pushed the cart toward the checkout stand and they stood in silence as the cashier rang them up. He wanted to talk to her to ask which *he* she meant—her ex or the horse—but as they pushed the cart through the parking lot, it clanged and jingled so loudly on the asphalt that he would have had to yell to be heard over the sound.

He slid the board into the back of the truck and looked back at Whitney as he pushed the cart to the front of the store. There was something she wasn't telling him. Something she feared, or was it something that she feared admitting to?

She was texting something on her phone as he got back into his truck. Before he could see what she was doing, she stuffed the phone into her pocket and out of his sight.

He got into the truck, sliding into the seat next to her. He started to open his mouth to speak, but thought better of it. If she wanted to talk, she could do so on her own time.

He knew better than most that some secrets were better left alone.

Chapter Nine

Whitney couldn't decide what she was more embarrassed about—falling all over the Christmas display, or falling all over her words and opening up to the one man she wanted to share her secrets with, but knew she couldn't. If she told him everything, he would be just as much in danger as she was. She couldn't protect everyone in her world; she couldn't even protect herself. And if Frank found her... This time she doubted that she would make it out of his grasp alive. She had only been lucky last time.

Her phone buzzed in her hand as her mother texted her. It was another one of her invitations to come home for Christmas, but they both knew that it wasn't an option. She kept asking where Whitney was and asking if she was safe, but the conversation only frustrated Whitney more. She couldn't tell her mother anything, and the loneliness and secrets were starting to get to her. She'd never been one to keep everything hidden, so she hated living this kind of life.

Colter was humming with the radio as he drove and she longed to reach over and take his hand back in hers again. It felt good to be touched again, and he clearly liked her. Yet she thought of the thousands of articles that she'd read in magazines and on the internet that talked about starting a relationship and dealing with stalkers. If Colter posted a picture of her online or said anything on Facebook, Twitter or any social-media site—it would only be a matter of time before Frank would track her down. She would have to run again.

She was so tired of running. So tired of hiding and the constant fear that came with it. And if she wasn't done running, no matter how badly she wanted a man like Colter in her life, she had to do what was best for both of them. And this time—it was just to let things go. He could find a woman who didn't have such a ridiculous amount of drama in her life. He could have a woman who wanted to get on a horse again. Or he could have a woman who was ready to simply start living again, who wasn't afraid of having her picture taken out of fear that the ghosts of her past would come back to haunt her. He could have a woman who was *safe*.

They parked in front of Pretties and Pastries, Sarah Rizzo's little café. Ever since her little accident at the hardware store, Whitney had nearly forgotten their other errand. Her stomach balled with nerves as she looked up at the pink-striped awning that sat over the front window of the café. The glass had a painting of Santa's workshop, complete with three little elves as they worked on parts of a train.

Everything about the caterer was too perfect for words. She owned a business. She could cook. Her hair was the perfect shade of blond. And unlike Whitney, she didn't have two little love handles around her waist when she sat down. Moreover, she didn't have drama.

Whitney swallowed back her insecurities, or at least she tried to, but they crept up from the depths of her belly like tiny mites climbing up the leaves of a rose.

Sarah was the woman Colter should have been with. He had sworn that he didn't feel anything for the woman, and that she wasn't the one for him, but on paper even Whitney could see all the reasons he was wrong. Sarah had everything that a man like him, a man who was stable, could want.

"Do you want to wait in the truck?" Colter asked, motioning toward the oh-so-cute shop.

What she wanted was to be back in the confines of her office, safe and secure and not overwhelmed by the confusing mess of emotions she was feeling, but since that wasn't an option and she was forced to face reality… Well, she had to make the best of it. That started with her facing the fact that there were other women in the world who wanted to be with Colter. As his friend, she couldn't be jealous or possessive of him. She needed to point him in the right direction, even if that meant pointing him toward Sarah Rizzo.

He needed to realize that maybe the pretty chef really was the best fit for him, but he would never do that if he thought there was something between Whitney and him.

In the fight between her head and her heart, she needed to let her head win this one—even if it went against everything that she felt and wanted to continue to feel.

"No, I'll go in with you. I should pop in and say hello to her at the very least," she said, forcing herself to smile.

He frowned as he looked over at her, but no matter how long he looked, she was sure that he would never start to understand exactly what she was thinking. Men were smart, but they were never going to understand women.

"Okay." He drew the word out as if it had more than two syllables. "We don't have to stay long." He grabbed the note his mother had sent for Sarah. Next to it on the dashboard was a red envelope, and as his finger brushed against it, he jerked back as though it had seared his skin.

For a second, she thought about staying behind and looking at whatever it was that had made him recoil from the letter, but she shook off the thought. Just like her, he was allowed to have aspects of his life that she knew nothing about.

He helped her out of the truck, their hands brushing against each other, but he didn't move to take her hand. She appreciated him not moving closer. It would make what she had to do that much easier if she didn't feel the heat of his skin against hers.

The door of the café opened with a jingle, and he stood holding it open for her to walk in. She took a long breath and stepped inside. The place smelled wonderful, like fresh bread and butter. It was warm and there were antique teapots and cups on shelves throughout the room. The place made her imagine a little English tea shop. It even had a kind of matronly air that was in direct contrast to the slim blonde who made her way out of the kitchen.

Sarah was wiping her hands on her apron. When she saw Colter she beamed, but as her gaze moved to Whitney, some of the brilliance in her smile faded. It was okay—Whitney could understand her disappointment. She had felt the same way when she saw Sarah with her arms wrapped around the man—it was a competition to her, a competition that no doubt she thought she was losing.

"Heya, guys," Sarah said. "How can I help you?"

Colter smiled. "My mother said she's been trying to reach you all day but couldn't get ahold of you. So she sent us here with a note about the menu." He handed her the piece of paper.

Sarah opened it, mouthing the words as she read. "Tell her that this shouldn't be a problem. I hadn't started to wrap the shrimp yet. I can make the change."

She stuffed the note in her pocket. "Do you guys want to come in and take a peek at everything?"

"No, we better get—" Colter started, but Whitney cut him off.

"Actually, that would be great," Whitney said, trying to sound far more excited than she was feeling.

"Okay." Sarah looked surprised and glanced over at Colter like she was trying to make sense of what was happening by reading his face.

She turned away and led them to the kitchen. Inside the doors there was a team of three young women. One was rolling dough, and the other two were making what looked like some kind of chocolate confections in the shape of horseshoes and Christmas trees.

"I was hoping to get as much done ahead of time as possible. That way I only have the final touches to do and put things in the ovens before heading out to the ranch." Sarah waved around the kitchen. There was a small table in the back. "Why don't you guys sit down?" She pointed toward the table.

Colter motioned for Whitney to lead the way, but from the way his body stiffened, she could tell he was deeply uncomfortable.

If he was that upset with her and Sarah being civil toward each other, and in the same room, then he had to feel more toward the woman than he was admitting to. The thought made a new tendril of jealousy grow through her. Even though Whitney had told herself this was what she had wanted, standing here in Sarah's den, it was harder than she had imagined.

It almost felt like she was the other woman, infringing on Sarah's territory.

Maybe Colter had been right and she should never have come in, yet there was no turning back now. She had to simply be strong and face her fears, even if it meant watching Colter being attracted to another woman.

Whitney sat down in the chair at the table with as much grace as she could muster.

"Let me grab us some plates," Sarah said. As she rushed around the kitchen, the other women looked over at her like she had lost her mind. "Oh, by the way, these are my cousins," she said, almost as if she had completely forgotten they were there until now.

"Nice to meet you," Whitney said, forcing herself to sound much happier than she was feeling.

Colter dipped his head in acknowledgment.

The cousins working on the chocolate whispered something to each other and they both started laughing as they glanced over toward her. Uncomfortable, she ran her hands over her hair, even though she was sure that what they were laughing at had nothing to do with what she looked like, but more to do with the man and the situation that she was in.

Sarah grabbed three plates and went to the stove and spooned meatballs out from the pot while Colter took a seat at the table. Opening the stove, she took out three twice-baked potatoes and plated them. She laid them on the table in front of them like they were in her home instead of in her shop and she was playing a welcoming host.

"I'm making these for the party. What do you think?" Sarah asked, clenching her hands together in front of her nervously.

Whitney followed Colter in taking a bite. She bit into the warm meatball, and its salty juices filled her mouth. It was delicious, and she popped another into her mouth. Sarah was a lot of things, and a good cook was at the top of the list. If the situation was different, Whitney would have loved to have her as a friend, a friend who could teach her the art of cooking.

"These are great," Colter said, motioning toward his missing bite of potato.

"Well done, Sarah. I'm totally impressed," Whitney said, wiping her mouth on a napkin.

"That's kind of you, Whit." Sarah lit up. "I feel like we got off on the wrong foot. I'm glad to see that I was wrong."

Whitney wasn't about to correct her and admit that whatever tension the woman had felt was real. This was her chance to fix things and be the bigger person, and who knew—maybe they really could end up becoming friends. Heaven knew she was a few short of a full quiver when it came to friends lately. And sometimes the unexpected friends were the ones who came to matter the most.

"Mom is going to love these," Colter said, filling

the tense silence between her and Sarah as she tried to come up with the right thing to say.

Sarah nodded. "I hope so. I'd love to keep catering your family's events."

"I can't think of a reason that wouldn't happen," Colter said, but he glanced over at Whitney like he was trying not to step on her toes.

"Do you all have big plans for your guests, Whitney?" Sarah asked. "I've heard good things about you from the people staying at the ranch."

"Well, bless your heart, Sarah. That's sweet of you to say," Whitney said with her best smile. "In the morning, we're gonna be taking the high-cotton guests out for a sleigh ride."

"High-cotton guests?" Sarah raised an eyebrow. "I've never heard that one before."

"You know… The ones who're living high on the hog."

"Oh, I get it," Sarah said, as she flipped back her hair. She took a bite of the meatball and swallowed it down. "Colter, I heard that there may even be a wedding or two coming up soon?"

Colter shifted in his chair and glanced toward her, before nodding. "Waylon and Wyatt are lucky men."

Whitney prayed that the woman wouldn't push the wedding talk any further. It made her want to sink into her chair, even though she didn't quite know why.

"Do you know when they are thinking about tying the knots?"

Colter shrugged. "There was some talk that they would do it over Christmas. You know, when all the family is home."

"Is Rainier getting out soon?" Sarah asked.

"Who's Rainier?" Whitney asked, feeling as though she was an outsider in their conversation.

Sarah laughed, but checked it just as quickly.

"Rainier is my youngest brother," Colter said, with a look of disbelief. "I thought everyone knew about him. My family always has a bit of drama, it seems."

"Especially lately, but I hardly think any of it is you guys' faults," Sarah added.

"Thanks," Colter said. "But I'm sure there are people in town who think otherwise."

"Well, I know just as well as you do that no one should be judged by the actions of their relatives," Sarah said, laughing as she motioned toward her cousins, who were obviously listening to the conversation but still pouring chocolate and working with the foods.

"Hey, now…" the woman closest to Sarah said with a laugh. "You ain't no saint, either."

Sarah nodded, looking over at Colter. "You're right… There are things that I am not proud of. But I'm sure we could all say the same, couldn't we?"

The statement made Whitney wonder exactly what they were talking about when it came to the perfect Sarah. Was there a side of her that she didn't know anything about? Were there as many skeletons in this woman's closet as there were in her own?

She doubted it.

Colter stood up, putting his napkin beside his empty plate. "I'll let my mother know about everything. And hey, thanks for the snack." His face was filled with an edge of panic at the reference to Sarah's past.

There had to have been more between him and Sarah than what he had told her. Whitney stood up, and picking up their dishes, she took them to the industrial sinks. "Yes, thank you," she said, relieved that the time had come for them to leave.

Sarah walked them to the front door as a couple made their way in. "If you guys need any other changes, it might be tough, but I'll try my best to make them happen. In the meantime, stay safe."

There was something ominous about the way the woman spoke, but Whitney tried to ignore the way it made the hair on her arms rise. She was seeing something that wasn't visible on the surface when it came to Sarah.

"Oh, and hey, Colter," Sarah called after them. "Don't forget to save me a dance!"

The door closed behind them. Whitney tried to stop from grinding her teeth at the woman's invitation. Now she had to be doing it to rub her friendship with Colter in her face. The woman should have known better—she had already won; she didn't need to keep coming after him.

"I'm sorry about that. You know you didn't have

to come in with me," Colter said, the words rushing from him.

She smiled. "That was fine. Sarah is nice."

"You think so?" he asked, watching her as if trying to gauge her reaction.

She couldn't give away anything that would make him see the jealousy and insecurity she was feeling. When it came to this, she had to stick to her guns—and what she knew was right, regardless of what she wanted. And the only thing that was right was for Colter to be with a woman who would fit in his life, not a woman he would have to help conceal from the hands of a madman.

Chapter Ten

Why did Sarah have to make everything awkward for him? After what felt like months of trying, Whitney was starting to open up and really talk to him, and then he found himself in the middle of some weird game he didn't understand. Whitney was staring out the window as they made their way toward the ranch.

The last place he wanted to be was back at the ranch. No doubt as soon as they hit the parking lot, Whitney would disappear and any progress they had made today would disappear right along with her.

"Do you want to go get some dinner or something before we get back?" He motioned toward the clock on the dashboard. "By now they've all eaten dinner. We're going to be on our own."

Whitney looked at him with a soft, placating smile on her lips. "We just ate at Sarah's."

"Right," he said, chastising himself for such a stupid idea. "But that wasn't a lot of food. You have to still be hungry."

She gave a resigned shrug, and the motion was so full of sadness that it made a pit open up inside him.

"There really isn't anything between Sarah and me, I promise," he said, trying to bring back the girl he had seen not an hour before—the bright, vibrant version of her that he loved so much.

"There should be something going on between you two—you're perfect for each other. You both have your lives together. My life…" Whitney threw her hands up in the air. "There's nothing about me that you should be attracted to. I have nothing to offer you. Nothing like Sarah does. She's smart, funny, ambitious, and she clearly is into you."

"Don't compare yourself to her. You are nothing like her," he argued.

"That's exactly my point, Colter."

"I meant that as a compliment. I mean that you're your own person. I don't know exactly what happened… you know, in Kentucky, but from what you told me, you are already stronger in my eyes than most women."

"How is running away strong?"

Was that what she had done—run away from home, from the man who'd tried to kill her?

"Is the guy still on the loose—your ex?"

Whitney looked over at him and he could tell by the set of her jaw that she was trying to decide whether or not she should tell him what she was really thinking.

"He got off with a slap on the wrist and credit for time served. In the end, even though he had burned down my family's barn and killed three prize horses, and nearly me—which is what he was after—he ended up only serving three months. You can read all about it on the internet. The jury decided that it wasn't premeditated—it was just some accident."

"But it wasn't?"

She shook her head and tears filled her eyes, but she wouldn't allow them to fall. "He wanted to kill me. He told me that he was going to. He locked the doors…" She took a deep breath. "I can still smell the smoke."

He knew the smell, that deep tarry scent of the world around him erupting into flames. He had dreams sometimes in which he was standing in the middle of a burning house without an exit—forced to face the flames and knowing that he would die. Yet he always woke up from the terror of his dreams. It was another thing to be standing there, in the middle of the flames, with nowhere to go and nowhere to hide.

"I knew that if I got out of the barn…he would be there waiting for me. Yet I had to try. I broke through the side of the wall near where the fire had started." She pulled back her sleeves. There, on the backs of her arms, were the telltale marks of third-degree burns. "I covered my face, but a piece of siding fell on me when I was running."

"Holy…" He reached over and ran his finger down the rough edges of her scar. She jerked at his gentle touch but didn't pull her arms away. "I'm so sorry, Whitney. I had no idea how bad…" He stared at the puckered pink scars on her arm.

"When I got back up, I could hear the sounds of Rudy in the barn. He was so scared. I ran to go back inside, but just as I got to the barn another piece fell—it knocked me out. And I…I let the thing I cared most about in the world die." Her voice was thick with her checked tears, and though they brimmed in her eyes, she wouldn't let them come.

"That fire. Rudy. None of it was your fault," he said, pulling the truck over to the side of the road so he could just talk to her. "Even if you could have gotten to your horse, the chances are that you would have been killed trying to get him out. You never go back into a burning building."

"But that's exactly what you do. Why is it so different for me to try and save something I loved?"

He moved closer to her and pulled her into his arms. She didn't resist; instead she put her head on his chest and let him hold her.

"Baby, what I do and what you did are two different things. I have gear. I'm trained to know how to read a fire's behavior. I know when and how it's safest to go about these things. And if the firefighters made it to your barn and didn't go in for the horses… then you have to know that you shouldn't have gone back in, either."

Her breathing was deep and he relished the feeling of her body against him. "I should never have left without him in the first place. I opened his stall, and the other horses', but he wouldn't come to me, and I went to open the barn door and found it locked. If I

had just grabbed him and made him come with me…
But I was…I was so scared. All I could do was just
stare at the door, praying that it would fly open and
we could all be free."

He didn't know what to say that could make her
feel better. He couldn't imagine all the things she
was feeling right now, but it was no wonder she had
gone just about as far away from Kentucky as she
could get.

"And Frank…" she continued. "I had a restraining
order filed against him, but just one week out of jail
he came back and came after me. Paperwork doesn't
stop hate. In fact, I think it only made it worse."

"Did he threaten you? What happened?" He tried
to stop the anger from filling his voice with hatred,
but even he could hear its hard edge.

She pushed her hair behind her ear and didn't say
anything. Instead she pressed her head harder against
his chest. "I can hear your heartbeat," she said.

"Answer me. Do you think he is going to keep
coming after you? Do you think he could know that
you're here, in Montana?"

She nibbled her lip. "I haven't told anyone where
I am, but you know as well as I do that if someone is
desperate enough—they will find you. I just want to
stay hidden as long as possible. Maybe he'll come to
his senses and fall in love with someone else. Maybe
he will realize that what he did is wrong."

"People like him don't change. He won't stop.

Sure, he may leave you alone, but you know he's just going to refocus his attentions to someone else."

"Or something else—like Dunrovin," she whispered.

"Do you think he's the one behind the floor—the bomb?" he asked, anger filling him with a fire of his own.

She shook her head. "If he wanted to come after me, he isn't coy. He drinks. That's what always starts it. He gets drunk and thinks he can take on the world. The next day, when he sobers up and realizes what he did, he comes around and apologizes. Then he feels bad and gets drunk again. It's a vicious cycle."

He ran his hand over his face as he thought about Frank coming after his family. He reached up and grabbed the red envelope off the dashboard. No one at the ranch, besides Whitney, knew the man. He flipped it over and, reaching around her, pulled the picture out. "Do you think he would have done something like this?"

She took the picture and stared at the faces before flipping it over. "'Mess with my family. I'll mess with yours,'" she said, reading the note on the back aloud. Her face looked paler in the thin moonlight that streamed through the front window of the truck.

Sitting up, she slipped the card back into the envelope and gingerly laid it back on the dashboard. After a moment she turned to face him. "I...I don't think he would do something like that. He wouldn't come after all of you—only me." She ran her hands over the knees of her jeans. "He never went after my parents. He is terrifying, but I don't think he wants to kill everyone who's ever been around me. I mean…" She motioned to the space between them. "You and I… We haven't even kissed. He couldn't know—"

So she was finally admitting that she felt it, too— the spark that always seemed to fill the air when they were near each other. He was glad he wasn't alone.

"That you're attracted to me?" he asked, with a teasing lilt to his voice.

She smiled. "I've said this a few times over the last few days, Colter Fitzgerald, but please let me remind you again—you are not God's gift to women. No matter what you think."

His laughter rang through the cab of the truck, and with its arrival some of the tension seemed to disappear and he was able to relax again.

"You say that, but your smile says something else," he joked.

She stuck out her tongue at him.

"My mother always used to tell me that if you stuck your tongue out, a bird would come along and poop on it," he said with a laugh.

"That's ridiculous. Plus, it's the middle of winter, at night, in a truck, and we're in the dark."

He lifted his hands in surrender. "Hey, it's just something my mom always said."

She laughed. "My mother always told me not to go to bed on an empty stomach," she said with a lift of her brow. "If you're still up for it, we could go somewhere… Get ice cream or something."

"Ice cream. In the middle of December?"

She shrugged. "We all have our vices—mine just happens to be ice cream and chocolate. Preferably, I like to have them together, but concessions can be made."

He laughed. "I always like a woman who knows her own mind but is willing to compromise when push comes to shove."

"Oh, and you know I would shove someone to get to Rocky Road."

It felt good just to laugh.

He turned the truck around and headed the couple of miles back to town. It had started to snow again, the tiny glittering flakes reminding him of a snow globe and how, even though his world had been shaken, it could still be beautiful in all its swirling chaos.

The town's other café, the Dew Drop, was closed, and the only Open signs on as they drove through town were in the steamy window of the bar and at the gas station just down the street.

"Do you ever feel like it's just not your day?" he asked with a laugh.

"What does that say, since you are hanging out with me?" She gave him a playful little shove.

"Trust me when I say that you are the best part of my day," he said, reaching over and resting his hand on the seat between them, waiting for her to slip her hand in his. "To tell you the truth, I didn't have to come to the ranch today. I knew my parents could handle whatever was thrown their way."

"So why did you come?" she asked, her voice playful and soft. She tiptoed her fingers across the seat to him and rested just the tips of her fingers in his open hand.

"Do I need to say it out loud?"

She smiled. "Well, I'd hate to assume something that I might have all wrong."

"What is it that you're assuming?"

She ran her fingers over the line of his palm as he pulled the truck into the gas station and parked. "I wasn't assuming anything," she said, her face catching the reds and blues of the neon lights that adorned the twenty-four-hour convenience store. "I guess I was just hoping that you had come to see me. I know it's a long drive from your house. And I'm sure you have better things to do."

He unclasped his seat belt, and leaning over their hands, he reached up and cupped her face. "When it comes to you, no distance is too much. I would travel across the world to be near you."

She leaned into his hands and closed her eyes. Her cheek was cool in his palm, and her skin was as soft as silk as he ran his thumb over the roundness of her cheek. He stared at her with her eyes closed, taking in the way her breathing slowed as she touched him, and the gentle curve of the tip of her nose. She was so beautiful. She had been the woman who had always come to him in his dreams, and he'd never known it until now.

He wanted to kiss her, but he simply watched her breathe, living in this moment as long as he could. As she gently opened her eyes and batted her eyelashes, she gave him a tiny smile.

"I don't know why, or how you feel the way you do...but I'm the luckiest girl in the world." She bridged the gap between them on the seat and climbed onto his lap.

He was taken aback by her as she straddled her legs around him. Leaning in, she took his face in her hands and looked him in the eye. "Whatever happens tonight, we're going to stay just friends. Okay?"

That was the last thing he wanted, but he knew if he didn't agree she would move away. He couldn't make that sacrifice. He had waited so long to have her like this...this willing and open.

"You agree?" she pressed.

He opened his mouth to say something teasing and noncommittal, but he couldn't find any words, so he finally just nodded.

She moved over him, rocking her hips. "No talk of relationships...and definitely not love. Love only makes things that much harder."

As the last word rolled off her lips, she leaned in and brushed her lips against his, making his body stir with the warmth of her breath and the unmasked lust of her words. He reached up and took hold of her hips, drawing her down onto him to let her feel what she was doing to him. If she wanted things harder, she needn't look any further.

She sucked in a breath, making the warmth of her kiss on his lips disappear. The loss was unacceptable and he took her mouth with his, flicking his tongue against her lower lip. He wanted to taste her…all of her. Yet she was in the driver's seat.

He chuckled at the thought.

She leaned back. "What?" she said, eyeing him with suspicion.

"Nothing," he said, his voice hoarse with want. "I just was thinking that maybe we shouldn't be doing this in front of the convenience store. You know, they have cameras." He pointed toward the tan camera that was pointed directly toward them. "In fact, I bet there's someone inside watching us right now."

She gave him an impish smile. "You want to give them a real show?"

Just when he thought he couldn't get any harder, she reached up and slowly unzipped her jacket.

"What do you think, Colter?" She let the coat slip from her shoulders, revealing her white sweater underneath. As she said his name, it was almost like it was coated with honey, sticky and sweet and full of the lifeblood of summer—a promise of life in the dead of winter.

"Anything you want, Whit… I'm yours," he said, reaching up and pushing a wayward piece of hair behind her ear.

He doubted the camera was in use anyway. In a

place like this, half the time the cameras were only for show. And in this moment, it was a risk he was willing to take.

Whitney slipped the coat from her and threw it onto the seat next to him. She turned and adjusted the volume on the radio and found a country station. "Tennessee Whiskey" was playing and her body moved with each heady beat. He'd always loved that song, but now...now it would be unforgettable.

She put her mouth against his earlobe and sucked as she reached down and unbuttoned his pants. Her hand was cool as she slipped it inside his jeans, and he gasped when she ran her fingers down his length. He tried to throw his head back with ecstasy, but her teeth grazed the skin of his earlobe, reminding him of who was really in control. Not that he needed a reminder. She could have as much control as she wanted...and he'd love every second of it.

He reached up under her sweater and felt the rough edges of lace as he skimmed over her bra. It made him ache for her even more. She stopped stroking him and pulled her sweater up and over her head and dropped it on top of her coat.

Seeing was even better than feeling. The lace was pink and it made him wonder if it was the same shade as her nipples. She shifted on him, and he moaned as his body shook with life. He ran his hands over her soft cream skin, taking in the lines of her waist and running his fingers under the waistline of her jeans. He slipped the button open.

Flipping back the edges of her pants, he found that the underwear matched. Either she was meticulous and the kind that planned out her outfit down to every little detail, or she had planned ahead. He liked the thought of her thinking about them like this, skating over the fine line between friends and into the realm of lovers.

He ran his hands up her sides. She was covered in goose bumps, but he wasn't sure if it was the chill of the winter that managed to penetrate the cab of the truck, or his touch, so he reached over and turned up the heat. To him, it already felt like a sauna, but he was sure that it had nothing to do with the temperature of the air around him, but rather everything to do with the heat of her touch.

He unclasped the hooks of her bra. She slowly let the straps drift down her arms, the pink lace bra teasing him as it trembled when she took the cups into her hands. Holding the bra in place, she slipped her arms out of the straps.

He longed to see her, to feel her naked body against him. To take her nipples into his mouth and taste her. He wanted it all, everything she had to offer.

He took her lips in his, letting her feel the need in his kiss and how badly he wanted this. Her. Now.

There was a rap on the driver's-side window.

"Oh, my God," Whitney said as she jumped off him, grabbed her sweater and pulled it over her head. "No. No. No."

Colter turned and wiped away the bit of condensation that had accumulated over the window. Standing beside the truck, in his full deputy uniform, was his brother Wyatt.

As he looked in, he smiled.

Behind him, sitting in an old beat-up blue Ford, was a man. His windows were frosted, but Colter could make out his greasy, long dark hair, bordering on black, and his weathered hands on the steering wheel. On the man's dashboard was a wooden bat.

Colter forced himself to look away from the man as he rolled down the window. The cold wind stole the warmth that his and Whitney's bodies had created. He cleared his throat and ran his hand over his hair, more out of instinct than the need to make sure everything was in place. "Yeah?" he asked, trying to sound far more innocent than he was feeling.

Wyatt leaned down and smiled at Whitney, who was slipping her jacket back on like nothing had happened. "You two having fun?" he asked, with a chuckle.

"We were until you showed up," Colter said, but he wasn't sure if he should admit anything or play dumb for Whitney's honor. He had never been the kind to kiss and tell, but he could hardly deny what they had been doing—and what more he had hoped for.

"I'm glad you were, but you do realize that you are being filmed." He pointed at the camera. "And even here, in Mystery, we have public indecency and exposure laws. And I was made to understand that the clerk, while he loves a good show, wasn't impressed."

"I doubt that," Colter said. "I'd bet my bottom dollar that the guy was just jealous."

"Be that as it may…" Wyatt said, smiling.

Colter raised his hands in surrender. "Won't happen again." As the words escaped him, he heard the mistaken finality, and as he glanced over at Whitney, she nodded. The smile she had been wearing disappeared, and with it, his hope for more.

Chapter Eleven

She could not have been more embarrassed. Her mother would have tanned her hide if she had found out what Whitney had just done and then given her a lecture on the merits of class and acting like a lady. Yet she was tired of being a lady all the time. She was tired of living within the strict confines that fear and heartbreak had placed around her—for once, she had stepped outside her comfort zone. Of course it had ended with her deeply shamed.

She felt more than stupid. If only she had gone with her original plan of just getting a little ice cream and she hadn't followed her heart instead.

Now she couldn't even look over at Colter without blushing. Though she was in her early twenties, it was like she was back in high school and heading home after a date. Yet this hadn't been and wasn't supposed to be a date...until she had pushed it there. If only she hadn't taken his hand, none of this would have happened.

There was no going back and undoing what had

been done, and there was no getting past the fact that not just one, but two of the Fitzgerald brothers, a cashier and possibly an innocent bystander had seen her in her underwear.

She groaned as she ran her hands over her face, like the simple action could scrub her mind of the thoughts running through it. There had been a million reasons she shouldn't have acted the way she did, yet she hadn't listened to any of them.

It was like she was back in Kentucky, dating Frank and not listening to the little voice in her head that had always told her to run—and yet she had stayed, up until the fire. It was only when her life had been in danger that she had finally found the strength she needed in order for her to follow the direction that her heart had been leading her toward.

She glanced over at Colter. He was gripping the steering wheel with both hands, squinting as he tried to see through the whitewash of snow in the headlights.

It was odd that her heart had led her to this place, this moment in time, and straight to him.

No. She had to be logical. Emotions be damned. She couldn't fall into the trap of the feelings. Desire and lust were fickle beasts.

Yet as she stared at him, she couldn't deny the fact that there was no being fickle when it came to Colter. And the way he had touched her… It had felt so good. He was a real man. The kind who took what he wanted, when he wanted it—and didn't wait to ask for permission. On the other hand, he wasn't forceful or bullish; being with him was like dancing. Each of their movements had been a complement of the other's, as if every motion were choreographed and perfected.

She could only imagine what he would be like if they ever ended up in bed together. She blushed at the thought.

"It's okay, Whit," Colter said, but he didn't take his eyes off the blinding snow as he drove. "Wyatt won't say anything."

She hadn't even thought of that. Wyatt seemed like a stand-up guy, but that didn't guarantee that the entire family and staff at Dunrovin wouldn't find out about their little escapade.

"Are you sure? And what if he saw something…?"

Colter smiled and shot her a naughty look, one that made her flush again—making her wonder if every time he looked at her she would have the same reaction. If she did, it would make work that much more challenging—which was the last thing she needed.

"We Fitz boys were raised to be gentlemen. If he did see something, which I doubt, no one will ever know it." He reached over and put his hand down between them again, but this time she vowed that she wouldn't take it, even though every part of her wanted to.

He wiggled his fingers, baiting her to take his hand, but she stood her ground and crossed her arms over her chest and forced herself to look out the window and into the night. There was something magical on nights like this, when the blizzard engulfed them, re-flecting the snowflakes in their headlights like bits of confetti. Though the world might have been telling her to celebrate, she couldn't join in.

"Are you mad at me?" He took hold of the wheel, giving up on her.

She glanced over at him and shook her head. "Not with you."

"Then with who?" He tried to win her over with his trademark grin, and though she melted with it, she didn't return his smile. "You know," he continued, "that cashier was probably just upset that you were with me. You are a beautiful woman. And if you think you're mad at him, trust me when I say that you can't be half as mad as me."

A giggle sneaked past her resolve. "I'm not mad at the cashier…no matter how jealous you think he is. Which, by the way, I think you are mistaken about."

"Then why are you upset?" he asked. "You aren't mad that you decided to kiss me, are you? I don't want you to regret that…ever."

"It's not you. It's just that I shouldn't have let things go there. It was a—"

Colter slammed on the brakes and she grabbed the dashboard to stop herself from slamming against it. The tires skidded on the icy road, twisting the truck in slow motion. He moved the steering wheel in a smooth circle the opposite direction of their slide, correcting the movement but sending the truck fishtailing in the other direction.

He threw his arm out, protectively holding her in place as he tried to control the truck.

Her stomach ached as they thudded to a stop against the snowbank the plows had left behind. This time of year they were so frozen that she wondered how much damage they'd done to the side of the truck.

"Are you okay?" he asked as he dropped his arm from her chest.

She nodded, but her body was numb thanks to the shock of the accident. "What about you?"

He ran his hands over his face, but nodded. "Did you see the horse?" he asked, motioning into the dark.

She hadn't been paying attention to anything except the swirling vortex of her thoughts.

"It ran out in front of us. I don't think I hit it, but we were close."

"What is a horse doing out in a snowstorm in the middle of the night?" she asked.

"I have no idea, but it looked like Clark."

"A ranch horse?" In the storm, she hadn't realized how close they were to the ranch. Though she had been driving up and down the roads leading to the place for months, in the darkness and snow she might well have been driving on the back side of the moon.

"Doesn't your mother check on the horses every night before she goes to bed?"

He nodded. "And she would have had them in the stables on a night like this. It's too cold."

"Are you sure it was one of ours? Your mother would never have left them out."

Colter's face pinched. "She wouldn't have, not unless something was very wrong."

He put the truck in gear and pressed on the gas, but the tires couldn't get the traction they needed to pull away from the snowbank and just spun in place. He tried to rock the truck back and forth, no doubt hoping it would afford him more traction, but the truck wouldn't budge.

He cussed under his breath, but she could tell he was trying not to show her that he was starting to panic. It snowed in Kentucky, some places averaging around two feet a year, so this was hardly the first time she had been stuck in a snowbank. Yet there was something about the night that suddenly felt ominous. Her thoughts moved to the bomb and the threatening note.

"You don't think someone did something to your mother, do you?" she asked, the pain in her stomach intensifying and bile rising into the back of her throat.

The lines around his eyes tightened and he set his jaw, making her wish she hadn't said anything. He had to have been thinking the same thing without her saying it.

"I'm sure she's okay," she said, trying to rectify her mistake. "Maybe the horses just got out or something."

"I hope so," he said, reaching into the pocket of his jacket and pulling out his phone. He scrolled through the numbers until she saw his mother's cell phone number pop up and he hit Call. He left it on speakerphone, and it rang until it finally gave up and went to voice mail.

"Don't worry," she said, trying to ignore the burn in her throat as she lied. "I'm sure she's just sleeping. It's the middle of the night, that's all."

"My mother always sleeps with her phone right next to her—just in case of emergencies like this."

As each second ticked by, she had to admit he was right—this was becoming more and more of an emergency.

"We're going to have to try and push the truck out," Colter said. "You slide over here and steer while I go around front and see if we can get her moving." He jumped out as she slid over into his seat.

She watched for him to give her the signal and she gunned it, revving the engine. The tires whirred against the ice and snow, and she could feel the truck rock as Colter pressed his weight against it, but they didn't move.

He pressed again and again, but each time the tires just slipped on the ice and their right tire dug deeper and deeper into the snow on the side of the road. Finally, he came around and got back in. His cheeks were red and there was a layer of sweat on his forehead as he took off his hat.

"Dang it," he said, half-breathless. "I was hoping that would work."

"How far are we from the ranch?"

Colter peered out into the night as though he were searching for some lights in the distance, but everything was under the veil of snow. "I'm guessing that we can't be more than a half mile. I mean, the horses…if they were in the barn…they couldn't have gotten too far. Right?" He asked the question like he was trying to comfort himself instead of looking for an answer, but that didn't stop her.

"Right," she said, trying to sound hopeful, but her attempt came out tinny and fake even to her own ears. "And who knows? Maybe they just walked over the fence thanks to a drift or something. You Montana boys get a lot of snow."

He tried for a smile, but it was just as forced and out of place as her attempt to comfort. "Let's go see if we can find the horses and round them up. If so, maybe we can ride them back to the ranch. You can ride, can't you?"

She had been riding her entire life, until recently, yet there was no way she could get back up on a horse—no matter how cold it was outside or how far they were from the ranch. She had no doubt in her ability to hike back, but horses… She couldn't risk being around them again. Just like men, they broke her heart—and all she did was let them down.

"I can't, Colter," she said, shaking her head. "But I can help you find them. Then you can ride back or something."

He looked at her like she had lost her mind. "It's not far, but that wind is cold and it's easy to get lost."

"But if we don't do something, who knows where the horses will be by morning? Is there any shelter out here, a wind block or something they can use to get out of the cold?"

Colter peered out into the night. "It's all pasture-land."

She nibbled at her lip. "As long as they aren't shivering, I think the horses will be fine. They should all have winter coats by now."

"Yeah, but my mother has been putting them in the barn every night. I don't know if they'd be up for this kind of cold. Plus, if we find them, we can get a ride home."

"First we have to catch them," she said, motioning outside to the flurrying snow.

He got out of his seat and reached behind the bench, grabbing a flashlight and handing it over to her. "Let's just stay together. The last thing we want is one of us getting lost in the dark. On a night like tonight, the cold has a way of sneaking up on you."

She took the flashlight from him and clicked it on as she stepped out of the warmth of the truck. "Don't they say that you should always stay with your car in cases like these—just to avoid hypothermia, Mr. Fireman?" she asked, only half teasing.

He chuckled. "In most cases, they would be right, but I think we have a couple of extenuating circumstances. Plus—don't forget—I'm a professional."

"Is that kind of like, *Hold my beer and watch this*?" she said with a laugh.

Colter nodded. "Exactly like that, except I have no intention of this ending in disaster."

She didn't want to mention the old adage that the road to hell was paved with the best of intentions. Besides, she'd already seen hell and it made this icy world look like a dream.

Chapter Twelve

They walked down the road, the world around them illuminated by the headlights behind them as Whitney called for the horse. The fresh layer of snow was littered with several sets of horses' tracks, making it look like there were at least five horses out.

"Clark couldn't have gotten far," Colter said. "And the others have to be close. They would stick together."

She nodded, sinking deeper into the warmth of her scarf as the cold night bit at her skin.

If there was more than one out, it didn't automatically mean foul play—horses always wanted to stay with their herd—but it was unlikely that one had just randomly gotten over or through a fence. Something else had to be at work, either a broken fence and an open barn, or someone had intentionally put them out. But why? Why would anyone let the horses loose?

By this time of night, everyone at the ranch had to be in bed and sleeping. If it hadn't been for them staying out late, no one would have known about the horses until the early morning feeding. Maybe, if someone was behind the horses being out, they had hoped the horses would go for a few miles and be harder to find. But why would they do something that was mostly just a nuisance?

On the other hand, they had scheduled rides with the guests in the morning. It was possible someone would know about their plans and would want to make them look bad in the eyes of their elite guests, but it seemed far-fetched.

Or maybe it was all set up to be some kind of distraction.

The world grew darker as they moved farther and farther away from the truck and its headlights, which were becoming two pinpricks in the night. The air around them grew colder, and as they walked, their boots squeaked on the snow.

"Mom would never put the horses out on a night like tonight—at least not without a blanket," Colter said, concern in his voice.

She had worked at the ranch for only a few months, but Eloise had always made sure that the horses were pampered. Colter was right that she wouldn't have put them out, but Whitney didn't want to make him even more worried than he already seemed to be.

"I just can't make heads or tails of this," he continued. "I mean, why would anyone go after the ranch's horses?"

They had told Sarah about their morning plans.

After they left, she would have had plenty of time to come out to the ranch and let out the horses without anyone seeing her. She had been somewhat catty, but it wouldn't have been in her self-interest to make a move against the ranch.

Then again, the move wasn't really against the ranch—maybe in Sarah's mind, this had been more of a move against Whitney. Maybe she was trying to make her look incompetent to the guests. She had to have known that she was the one who would have to deal with the clientele when things went haywire with their reservations and social events.

She thought back to the moment they had left the café—Sarah *had* seemed to threaten them. Maybe it hadn't been as idle as Whitney had assumed.

"Do you think Sarah—"

"Sarah what?" Colter asked, cutting her off.

The way he said her name made her back down. She had no proof, only a nagging feeling in her gut that she was missing something that was hiding in plain sight, something that tied all these mysterious events together.

"Do you know Sarah's family?" she asked, thinking about the ominous note.

"Not really. She and her family moved into town just a few years ago. One of her cousins married a Carter boy. I think they were from somewhere around Idaho."

He didn't have a relationship with her family, which seemingly put her out of the running—at least when it came to the note. Yet that didn't mean she still didn't have a hand in the horses being let out.

As they walked, the scent of wood smoke grew stronger. It carried the sweet smell of cottonwood and pine, and the smell reminded her of her winters in Kentucky. The aroma elicited thoughts of her family sitting around the Christmas tree, watching as the fire roared in the fireplace. Until now, she hadn't missed home.

She had loved waking up on Christmas morning to her mother's cooking. It had always been the same breakfast casserole—sausage, eggs, hash browns—all melded in the Crock-Pot overnight. And her mother's coffee… It had been so strong and dark that her father had made jokes about it having the power to melt the spoon.

Her mouth watered.

It was funny how one little smell could pull her back so far in time. Just like that, she was a child again, waiting impatiently for Santa to come and to make sure that she really had made it onto the good girls' list.

This year she was more unsure of her status on Santa's list than ever before. She had made so many mistakes. When she looked at herself and the woman she had been forced to become, it was almost as though she didn't even recognize herself. The things she had loved were merely memories now. Her home was no longer her home.

When Frank set that fire, he hadn't just made her

lose the things she had loved—he had also made her lose herself. And that was just as impossible to bring back. She'd never be the same girl she had once been. She'd never be carefree again. She had seen the underbelly of humankind, the dark sickening world of those who, simply put, just weren't right in the head.

Almost as if he could read her mind, Colter slipped his gloved hand in hers. "You warm enough?"

She moved her fingers between his. Though she was wearing thick wool gloves, the tips of her fingers had started to go numb and she basked in the warmth of his touch. "I will be." She smiled. "I was just wishing that maybe we had gotten that ice cream."

He stopped. "I hope you don't regret anything. You know…"

She didn't regret getting into trouble with him, not entirely anyway. It had been a long time since she had felt that nibble in her belly and the need to be touched the way he had touched her. "Nothing like that," she said, squeezing his fingers. "I'm just hungry." As if on cue, her stomach growled.

"Are you saying you wish you would've gone for the ice cream instead?" he teased.

"Never, but I am starting to pretend that the snow is marshmallow fluff. Don't worry about me if I dive in headfirst here in a minute or two."

He laughed as they started to walk again. Her flashlight bobbed around, lighting the way in front of them, and occasionally she flashed it around in the darkness. As she moved it to the right, she caught the shining reflection of a large set of eyes.

"Clark, baby," she cooed, squeezing Colter's fingers and motioning toward the horse in the distance. "Do you have anything, a halter or a lead or something?"

Colter shook his head. "I'll just climb up. You can ride with me."

Just the mention of her riding made her blood pressure rise and her heartbeat begin to thunder in her ears. There was no way…no way she could get on the back of the horse. Yet she didn't want to let him down.

She stepped off the road, carefully picking through the deep drifts of snow as she worked her way slowly to the horse. A part of her wanted the horse to spook and for them not to be able to catch him, but if they didn't get him and he tore off into the night, they would lose track of him—or spend all night trudging around in the open fields in the freezing cold.

Clark threw his head and pawed at the snow as they neared him. He was shivering, and the whites of his eyes were visible as she grew nearer. He must have still been scared after his close run-in with the truck.

"Don't move too fast," Colter said, stepping beside her. "If he runs off, we're going to have a long walk back to the ranch."

If they didn't get their hands on the horse, the cold was going to make the midnight trek nearly unbearable. As it was, even though she had been prepared for the cold, her toes were starting to ache. She was tough, but there was no amount of toughness that could prepare someone for below-zero temps made colder by the harsh chill of the wind.

The wind… She turned around. Her tracks were already beginning to get filled in thanks to the drifting snow. If they didn't get to the horse and start back, their footprints would soon be nearly indistinguishable from the natural dips and valleys in the dark.

She hadn't been really scared about their safety… until now, with the full reality of the whipping snow blasting against her face. In an instant, this could become a fight for their life.

Maybe this was what someone had planned on all along—maybe they'd known full well that she and Colter would find the horses and be forced to go out into the night to wrangle them. And maybe they hoped that they would get lost and be found as ice cubes in a snowbank somewhere the next day.

She brushed off the thoughts. She was being absurd. No one could have expected anything. Horses were horses. They were always just a bit mischievous. No doubt Clark was probably the ringleader in the escape. Maybe they had been spooked by the storm. Maybe someone forgot to close the barn and they had simply walked over the fence.

Not everything bad that happened was meant to threaten them or the ranch. Sometimes bad things just happened. And nearly everyone who had ever owned a horse had had them break loose at least once. It was in their nature to want to be free.

She stuck her hand out, hoping to entice the horse to come to her. Clark took a few tentative steps, but threw his head again as he caught her scent.

"You try," she said to Colter, hoping that the horse would pick up his scent and it would make him feel safer.

This horse, this beautiful black gelding who looked so much like Rudy, wasn't her beloved boy. To this horse, she was nothing more than a stranger who wasn't to be trusted. Yet, if the horse was like her, he would have realized that it wasn't the ones whom you didn't know that did you the most harm.

Colter moved slowly toward the gelding, his head down. "Hey, handsome boy," he said, his voice comforting but strong. "How'd you get out, baby?"

The horse shivered, drawing in a long breath and huffing a greeting to him.

"Good boy," Colter said, coming close and lifting his hand.

Clark took a hesitant step toward Colter's hand and let him slip his fingers under his mane. Colter smiled as he stroked the horse. "That's a man," he said, walking around the horse's body. He leaned against the horse and, in one fluid motion, lifted himself up and onto Clark. The horse looked back, giving the man a side-eye and taking a step forward.

"Hey, now, Clark," Colter said, "I didn't tell you to get moving. We have to pick up our rider, man."

Clark stopped, shifting his weight.

"He's voicing his complaint," she said with a giggle.

"He isn't one who likes to be bossed around—not that I know anyone else who is like that or anything," he teased.

"Hey, I'm a fine employee. I have no idea where you got that idea," she joked.

"I wasn't saying anything about you as an employee. My mother loves you. I just happen to know that you aren't the kind that is ever going to let someone push you around against your will."

Her thoughts instantly went to Frank, and her heart sank. She had let him push her around, not physically, but emotionally, for too long. She had been all too acquiescing when it came to him and what he had wanted. Yet, since she had come here, she had changed. Maybe Colter was seeing her as she wanted the world to see her—strong, uncompromising and brave.

Was that who she had truly become or was it nothing more than a show?

If she ever had to face Frank or a man like him again…she doubted that she could keep up this strength or bravery. She would probably fall to her knees and beg for mercy. She could never go back to being the girl in the barn—the girl who had hoped to survive. In fact, she couldn't help wondering if in her survival she had already used up all her lucky stars. Next time, if there were ever a next time, she doubted that she would have the strength or good fortune to survive.

Colter stuck out his hand, motioning for her to take it so she could climb up behind him.

She took a step back. "I'll just walk. It'll be fine."

"It's going to be at least a mile. If you sit up here with me, you can snuggle close and I can keep you warm," he said, his playful grin taking over his face.

She knew it didn't make any sense, her fear of riding. And really, it wasn't the act of getting back on the horse that bothered her. It was just, for her, that the act of riding was a way of bonding with an animal—it was the smooth motion of her thighs against its back as they worked in tandem. It was a promise the rider made the moment she got on to take care and treat the horse with kindness and do nothing that was against the horse's best interest, and more than anything, it was just the feeling of being up there that she feared the most. If she got up, it would be like being on Rudy again.

It would bring up far too many memories…and even more disappointments.

If she got up on Clark, there was a good chance it would open her heart to things that it just wasn't ready for. It was just too risky.

Being with Colter had already made her more vulnerable than she had intended to be when she came here. Only time would tell if her opening up to him would be a mistake. She couldn't give any more of herself when she couldn't be sure that she hadn't made the wrong choice.

"Colter, I'm not ready."

He closed his hand and laid it on his thigh, nodding. "Okay. If that's the way you feel, I understand."

She wanted to think that he meant what he said, and he really understood the way she was feeling, but a part of her doubted it. He couldn't understand what it was like to experience what she had been through. He couldn't understand the way her chest constricted at the mere thought of riding again, and the way the scent of the fire would spring to the front of her mind when she had gone near horses. He couldn't understand the trauma. No one could—she herself barely did.

She turned away from Colter, afraid that he would be able to see the pain in her face if he looked at her. He needed to see her as emotionally strong and nothing else.

Colter rode up beside her and she walked next to the horse and rider until they made it back to the road and started heading east in the direction of the ranch. As they started down the road, there was the crunch and nicker of the other horses as they caught up. Looking behind them, she saw the line of four other horses nose-to-tail as they walked in the trail Clark and Colter had broken in the snow. She was moving at a slower pace than the horses, but Colter kept them in step with her.

The horses looked tired and the palomino was

shivering as the wind whipped against her. They needed to get the horses back. Though they would likely have been okay in the cold, it made her cringe watching them combat the elements.

Pellets of snow pelted against her face as the snow started to fall harder with each footstep. Though she was dressed for the weather, her fingers had grown so cold that she couldn't feel her fingertips and she bumbled as she moved to wipe her nose, bumping her fingers against her cheek.

She could feel Colter's gaze as she moved, and even more, she could feel his concern. He pulled Clark to a stop and got down. He took off his scarf and wrapped it around Clark's neck, using it as a lead rope.

"You can ride. I'm doing fine," she said. She motioned toward the bit of Christmas lights that were glowing in the distance. "We're almost there."

He took her hand, and his warmth burned through her gloves like he was on fire. He frowned as he must have felt the chill. "No, you're not," he said, lifting her hand to blow on her fingers.

They ached as the heat of his breath moved over her nearly frozen skin, but it wasn't her hands that came alive with his touch and his kindness; rather, it was her heart.

Chapter Thirteen

Everything last night had gone wrong. Until they had gotten back to the ranch and found his mother and father warmly tucked in their bed. He hadn't bothered to wake them up when he found out that they were safe and sound.

He hadn't been that scared of losing his parents in a long time. That fear of what could possibly have happened to them had brought up so many memories of when he'd been young and his biological parents had left him alone. He'd always thought they were never coming back, that something bad had happened—until the last night he had spent with them, and his father had left him on the fire department's doorstep. As a child he had often wondered if all that worry had caused all the bad that had come of them—almost as though he had wished it upon his parents.

He had given up the thoughts of a boy. He had finally found some reprieve thanks to his new life and the realization that he wasn't in control of anyone else's destiny but his own. He hadn't caused his parents to leave him, he hadn't caused their addiction or neglect, and he couldn't cause his parents to be hurt just because he had secretly wanted them to disappear.

Yet, last night, that fear had returned—as though perhaps his curse had returned and because he had even voiced the possibility that his mother had been hurt. He had half expected to find her on the floor, and the illogical thought made goose bumps rise on his arms.

Colter shook his head as he went out to the barn and looked in on the horses. Two of the escapees were poking their heads over the doors of their stalls and they nickered as he grabbed a handful of pellets and made his way over to them.

"You rebel," he said, feeding the mare, Jingles, a pellet. As she nibbled at his hand, looking for another, he scratched her forehead. "At least one of us got a little sleep, I hope."

The horse stopped nibbling and looked up at him, and he could have sworn that she was laughing at him.

When they'd gotten back to the barn, they found the door open and the stalls unlocked. Though they had questioned everyone at the morning meeting, no one had come forward and admitted to any wrongdoing—not that he had expected anyone to, especially with his mother in the state she had been in.

There was only one other time he had ever seen her so mad, and it was the day that Rainier had been arrested.

The barn door opened behind him with the familiar sound of grinding metal.

A dark-haired man about sixty, his hair slightly too long and pulled back into a tight man bun, poked his head inside.

"Can I help you?" Colter asked, not recognizing the man as an employee but he had seen him somewhere before.

"I was just looking for Sarah. Is she around?" the man asked, his voice the throaty rasp of a smoker's.

"Sarah…Sarah Rizzo?" he asked. "The caterer?"

The man nodded. "She asked me to meet her here today about a job."

"Why would she want to meet you here?"

The man shrugged. "Look, buddy, I was just doing as I was told."

"What's your name?"

"If Sarah isn't in here…" The man ducked out of the door without bothering to answer Colter's question.

He rushed after the stranger. "Wait up!"

The man was halfway across the parking lot, on his way to the ranch office, before Colter caught back up with him. "Stop, man. What's your name?"

The man stopped and turned to face him. "The name's Daryl."

"Daryl what?" Colter pressed.

The man looked toward the office almost as though he wished he had walked a little bit faster so he wouldn't have had to answer any of his questions. "It's Daryl Bucket."

The name rang a bell. "Do I know you?" Colter stared at the man and the way his mouth puckered at his question, making the fine smoker's lines around his lips deepen.

Daryl shrugged. "Who am I to go on and say who you know and who ya don't?"

Was this the kind of guy who was really coming to Sarah in hopes of getting a job? What did he plan on doing—pissing people off?

"I don't think Sarah's here. I haven't seen her to—"

"In that case, I'll just go on into the office and wait for her." The guy motioned to Whitney's office.

The last thing Colter was going to do was leave this guy alone with her. Not on his life. "Why don't you just move along? I'll tell Sarah that you stopped by."

The guy smiled. There was something dangerous about the way his lip quivered over his stained yellow teeth. "I don't know who you think you are, man, but I need a job. I've been a trucker all my life and things dried up. It's the holidays. I got bills rolling in that need to be paid. I ain't gonna screw this chance up."

The dude could play at his heartstrings all he wanted, but with things like this, Colter always trusted his gut, and it was warning him that there was more to the guy than what he was telling him.

The door to the office opened up, and his father,

Merle, and Whitney walked outside. As his father saw the man, his face lit up. "Daryl, is that you, old man?"

Daryl smiled, the motion losing its dangerous edges as he looked over at Colter's father.

"What are you doing here?" his father asked as he and Whitney made their way over to them.

"I was hoping to get a job with your party's caterer. She wanted to meet me here when I told her about you and I." The man looked over at Colter. "Your man here was giving me a hard time."

Colter's dad looked over at him and gave him a wink. "Oh, he can be a tough one when it comes to strangers. We tried to train it out of him, but, well... you can see how well that worked out."

Daryl gave him the side-eye.

"Mr. Fitz, this poor gentleman is going to think you're serious," Whitney said, coming to Colter's rescue.

He gave her a smile, but as he looked at her, he couldn't quite catch her gaze. He couldn't be sure if she was intentionally avoiding his eye or not, but he hoped for the latter. They had moved quickly last night, but he didn't want her to regret it. For him, their time together was something special, and something he wanted to repeat, but if he had another chance he'd love to see it to completion.

"Just joshing you, Daryl," Merle said, slapping the man on the shoulder. "This is my son Colter— the fireman."

Daryl's eyes widened with surprise and he stared at him, not speaking for a minute.

"Nice to meet you, officially," Colter said, attempting to mend the broken fences between them for his father's benefit.

"Yeah, likewise," Daryl said, but he looked Colter up and down like he was trying to figure him out.

"Daryl used to work at the ranch when we were first starting up. It's been a long time. Hasn't it?" Merle asked.

Daryl nodded but didn't really say anything, nor did he look too happy.

"Daryl did a great job teaching me how to use the heavy equipment and getting the ranch up and running."

"I always had a connection to this place," Daryl said.

"As you can see," Merle said, motioning to the world around them, "we made things work. Couldn't have done it without you."

Colter's father might have liked the guy, but that didn't mean he had to.

Thankfully, Sarah drove up in her black this-year's-model Chevy truck and got out. She waved as she walked over. Everyone stared at her, the seconds ticking by as slow as cold oil dripping out of its jug. He tried to ignore the dread that crept through him with each of her nearing steps.

"Heard you all had a little bit of a rodeo when you all got home last night," Sarah said with a laugh.

"Nothing we couldn't handle." Whitney's face pinched, but she forced a smile. "How'd you hear about it all so fast?"

Sarah waved her off. "Oh, you know nothing that exciting can go too long without hitting the phone tree. Your mom had business this morning with Ms. Babinski, who called her sister, who called Mrs. Long, who called me."

It was a wonder anything ever stayed private in their little town with an information dissemination system as active and on-it as the women of Mystery.

"What happened last night?" Daryl asked, making Colter feel at least a little bit better in the knowledge that not everyone in the town knew every one of their movements.

"They near ran into one of our horses who, along with his comrades, managed to escape. Got run off the road," Merle said. "They're damn lucky that they made it home before they froze their buns off. Weatherman said with the wind chill it was nearly forty below last night."

"Were the horses okay?" Daryl asked, looking toward the barn.

For the first time since he'd met the guy, Colter actually found something to like about him.

"Yeah, they are all fine. Luckily, they had pretty good coats going, but they were all a little out of sorts this morning, so we gave them a little extra hay."

Daryl nodded his approval.

"What are you doing here, Sarah?" Whitney asked.

Colter was sure that she hadn't intended to sound suspicious, but her tone was less than cordial. After their taste testing at the shop, he had thought things between the two women had started to get better, but on their walk back, Whitney had asked about the woman's family—making him wonder if she suspected that Sarah was in some way involved in the horses' escape.

He looked over at her and Sarah sent him her best dazzling smile and a lift of the brow as though she had heard the implication in Whitney's tone, as well. Sarah was conventionally pretty, skinny and blonde, what most guys would call stacked thanks to her ample upper assets, but she wasn't his type. However, no matter how much he tried to convince Whitney, the more she seemed to dig her heels in when it came to believing him. He could hardly wait for Yule Night to be over so he wouldn't keep running into the woman, but without the coming festivities it also meant he had less of a reason to keep popping in at the ranch—and seeing Whitney.

"I have a few interviews this morning," Sarah said, her tone almost questioning. "I just thought your boss, Mrs. Fitzgerald, would want to weigh in on my selection." She turned to the man standing next to Merle. "I assume you are Daryl?" She stuck out her hand and Daryl gave it a tight and swift shake. "Why don't we head to Mrs. Fitz's office? I know she's going to be waiting for us."

Merle glanced down at his watch. "If you don't

mind, Colter, I'm going to talk with Daryl. I'll take a hand to go and get your truck in a bit."

Whitney looked as though she was literally biting her tongue as Sarah, Merle and Daryl made their way toward the house.

"Sarah, wait!" Whitney called after her. She gave Colter an apologetic tip of the head, but turned and walked toward the woman.

Sarah stopped, motioning for the men to go ahead. "Can I help you?" She put her hand on her hip as she turned to face them.

Colter followed Whitney, and the dread he had been feeling intensified. Whatever Whitney was planning on doing with Sarah, it wasn't going to play out well. He could feel it in his toes. There was just too much tension between the two women for any progress to be made. He wished he could just make them both stop. There was enough going on at the ranch without him having to stand between the two women.

Whitney stopped just out of the woman's reach. "What did you do after we left your shop last night?"

"What? Why?" Sarah asked, looking to Colter as if asking him to help her decipher Whitney's sudden line of questioning.

In all truth, Whitney's suspicion had gotten him thinking, and after he kissed her good-night he'd gone back to his place and had tossed and turned all night as he tried to come up with a list of possible suspects. Sarah didn't seem to entirely fit the bill, but no one he had thought of really did, either.

He knew it was naive, but the only thought that had finally allowed him to get some sleep was the hope that all these little incidents would simply come to a stop. Perhaps whoever had left him the threatening picture would come to realize that this wasn't a fight worth having.

"Colter, are you really going to let your little secretary treat me like this? I've been nothing but good to your family. I can't imagine what she is trying to get at," Sarah said, motioning toward Whitney.

He was pretty sure he could almost see the steam rising from Whitney as her face pinched into a tight scowl at the woman's questions. "Look, Sarah. You're right. You've been great to work with so far. We've just been running into a few *things* that are a bit strange and worrying. If you'd just tell her where you were last night after we left, then we'll be along. No big deal. We just want to make sure that we cross all the innocent people off our list."

"How big is your list?" Sarah asked. "Only me?"

He scuffed his boot against the grit they had put down on top of the ice in the parking lot. "Where were you, Sarah?"

She huffed. "I was working on getting the appetizers together last night. My cousins and I were there until about ten and then we went home."

"Did you go home alone?" Whitney pressed.

"What is that supposed to mean?" Sarah asked, affronted. "Do you think I'm going home with random men? What do you know about your little friend here, Colter? Has she told you who she really is? About her past?"

He looked over at Whitney. Her jaw was clenched tight and her face was red, but he doubted that it was because of the cold. "This isn't about Whitney and her past. This is about you and where you were and who you were with. Don't try to deflect, Sarah."

"This is crazy, Colter. And if you don't see that, then you deserve to be with a woman like her—one with a closet full of skeletons…and not just the figurative kind." Sarah pointed toward her. "I don't know what she has you thinking about me, but all I care about is my business and my family."

Whitney gave a derisive snort. "How did I know you would say something about your family? You say you're innocent…but it's strange how everything we know about the suspect points straight toward you."

"What's in this for you, Whitney?" Sarah asked, turning toward her so their faces were only a few inches apart. "Do you think you can come here and stir up trouble in hopes that it will make people forget about who you really are? What you did? I know all about you—and how you falsely accused your boyfriend of starting a fire in your barn… All so you could get the insurance money. You should be in prison."

"You don't know what you're talking about," Whitney said, the color draining from her face. She looked toward him. "Don't listen to her. I promise it's not like she said. I had nothing to do with that fire."

"From what I heard, she staged the whole thing," Sarah said, looking to him with self-righteous indignation. "If you were smart, you would have her hit the road before a mysterious fire breaks out here. Dunrovin doesn't need any more trouble—especially her kind."

Chapter Fourteen

Whitney stormed off, bumping against Sarah as she made her way to her office, and slammed the door. He thought about going after her, but he'd learned long ago that sometimes the best thing he could do when it came to dealing with an angry woman was to give her a few minutes to collect her thoughts. And he still had Sarah to deal with.

"That was cruel, Sarah," he said, though he could think of several more colorful words he could have used instead of *cruel*.

She looked at him, her eyes brimming with angry tears. She looked like a broken woman. "You don't think I *wanted* to call her out like that, do you?" she asked, motioning after Whitney. "She just made me so angry. I wouldn't do anything to hurt this ranch or stand in the way of its success. Your success means my success. Just like everything else in this community, we are all interconnected. A rising tide raises all boats, you know?"

He believed there was some validity to what she

had to say, but the way she was fighting so hard and throwing such low blows made him wonder if there weren't some things she was hiding as well—things that Whitney had brushed against, and had caused the woman to lash out.

"Did you go home alone last night?" he asked, his voice as soft and understanding as he could make it.

She sucked in a breath. "The only person I want to go home with is you, Colter." She reached out and took his hand.

Her touch felt foreign, cold and unwelcome even though she was wearing thick black gloves. She squeezed his fingers, but instead of returning her affection, he pulled out of her grasp. "That's not a good idea, Sarah." He couldn't look her in the face. He hated this moment, when people weren't at the same emotional place. It always made things so awkward. "You are a great gal, but I'm—"

"Dating her?" Sarah interrupted, finishing his thought.

He nodded. "She's pretty amazing, regardless of what you seem to think about her."

"You are being stupid, Colter. You are passing on someone, me…a woman who has her life together, all so you can play house with her. She is nothing but trouble." She looked up at him, anger filling her eyes. "You're going to regret this."

The hairs rose on his arms at the threat in her tone. "What do you mean by that, Sarah?"

"Really?" She sneered. "I can't believe you." She

turned around and stormed off, but turned back and pointed at him. "You are going to call me and apologize when everything between you and her goes to hell. And I'm going to tell you that I told you so. Mark my words."

She stomped into the house, slamming the door behind her.

There seemed to be a lot of that kind of thing happening in his life right now. He hadn't said anything to start this, yet here he was, dealing with a potentially dangerous suspect, who was coming after his family, and two women who wanted to have him chase after them.

Luckily, the repairing of the loft's flooring waited.

He walked back to the barn, making sure to close the door to keep some of the residual warmth from the animals from getting lost to the cold. Clark looked over at him, smacking his lips as though asking for a pellet.

"Keep wishing, you little rebel," he said, but the horse made some of the tension in his shoulders dissipate.

The horse threw his head, nickering a response that he didn't have to guess too hard to know was a rude comeback.

"That kind of talk isn't gonna get you what you want, old boy," he said, with a slight laugh.

He walked over to the bench. Hanging on the wall above it was a collection of farrier tools, scissors, hoof picks and the like. His stress was nothing a little hammering wouldn't help bring back under control. He grabbed the supplies he'd need and the board and made his way up to the loft. One of the horses huffed and stomped, and there was the shuffle of hooves and heavy bodies as he carefully stepped around the hole in the floor.

He put down his supplies and ran his finger along the rough, saw-cut edge of the floor. It still didn't make any sense to him why someone would have done this. Merle had been the one who intended to come up here to get the decorations. Which meant that someone must have been coming after him, but Colter's father was one of the most likable people he knew. Sure, he was quiet and a bit stoic with people he didn't know, but if anyone needed anything he would be the first person there to lend a hand.

His mother was the same way.

This all must have had something to do with the threat—they really were targeting members of his family, yet none of his brothers or their significant others had mentioned anything suspicious or off-putting to him. Then again, he hadn't mentioned any of this to them, or their parents, either. Maybe they were trying just as hard as he was to make sure everything kept running smoothly.

He wouldn't have put it past them, to try their best to keep a secret of that magnitude. They had all been through enough over the years that when push came to shove they would all do whatever it took to make sure the people they loved were safe. It was the one thing they all had in common—aside from their love of animals.

Picking up the box of wood screws, he let it slip from his cold fingers and crash to the floor, spilling its contents all over. Several of them rolled off the edge of the rough-cut hole in the floor.

"Son of a nutcracker," he said with a grunt as he caught more from falling into the hole.

He didn't need them getting into the pellets bin below. If one of the horses got a screw, he'd never get over the guilt.

He scooped the screws into the box and, getting up, made his way over to the boxes where several had rolled. On top of the box closest to him was a green cap with a red star on it. It was the kind that could be found on a beer bottle. He picked it up, flipping it over in his fingers.

When he looked up, something green caught his eye from in the shadows behind the box. He moved the box. Behind it were three empty green beer bottles. The same kind of bottles as the one he had found near the cattle guard.

Beside the bottles was an old, grease-smattered towel. Several pieces of it were gone, and a piece had been ripped free and was sitting near one of the bottles.

He moved another box, bumping it against something. He stepped carefully over the green bottles, not touching them as he moved. There, sitting in the darkness, tucked behind another box, was a plastic gas can.

He took out his phone and dialed. Wyatt answered on the first ring.

"Hey, brother. How's it going?" Wyatt said, sounding glad to hear from him.

He hated to ruin someone else's day as well, but he needed to bring him in on this—he couldn't let something else happen if he could stop it. "I need you at the ranch. Are you close?"

"I was just leaving my house. What's going on?" Wyatt asked, the excitement leaching from his voice.

It didn't take Colter long to tell him about his findings and the events over the last few days—including the picture.

Ten minutes later, there was the screech of metal as Wyatt entered the barn, phone still in hand. "I'm up here," Colter said, with a nod.

"Why didn't you tell me about all this before?" Wyatt asked, stuffing the phone into his pocket. "I can't believe you, of all people, would allow this kind of thing to go on for this long without getting me involved. It was stupid, Colter. Stupid as hell. Who knows what this person is capable of."

Colter sighed. He should have known this would be how Wyatt would react. He had always been a little bit of a pessimist when it came to human nature, while Colter had always been more of an optimist. Up until now and the recent events at the ranch, Colter had thought his brother was wrong—that living a life focused on the evils that another could do was unhealthy. Yet now he had to admit that maybe that kind of thinking was better for a person. At least you could be prepared when the worst happened.

"You know, Colter, someone could have gotten hurt."

Someone had already gotten hurt and her name was Whitney, but he wasn't ready to tell his brother about their relationship and all the things he'd come to learn about her and her past. His brother would immediately want to ask him questions—questions he wasn't sure he was ready to answer, at least not without talking to her again. Especially after Sarah's accusations.

They had shaken him. He was sure Whitney had told him the truth about her past and all the things that had happened in Kentucky, but from the way Sarah had spoken, there was more to it than what Whitney had told him.

He pushed the thoughts from his mind. Whitney wouldn't have lied to him. No. She wasn't the kind. And who knew where Sarah had come across the information? Probably from Facebook or something equally as unreliable.

"Why can't you take anything seriously, Colter?" Wyatt asked, coming down on him full force.

"This has nothing to do with me not taking things seriously. I'm taking this as seriously as a heart attack. I just thought I could handle it," he said, trying to make his brother understand.

"You thought you could single-handedly take on a potential killer? What were you thinking?" Wyatt took out his camera and started snapping pictures of the bottles and the scene. "Something like this could go federal… Did you ever think about that? Can you imagine if the FBI found out that there was someone potentially making bombs at the ranch?"

"I'm not stupid, Wyatt," Colter said, picking up his saw and cutting the hole square so he could fit the board into place and taking a minute to cool off before he said something he regretted.

Wyatt was just upset. He had every right to feel the way he did about Colter concealing the truth. He would have been pissed if his brother had done the same thing, but Wyatt had to understand that there was more to all this than just a secret.

Colter set down the saw as he finished his cut. "I was fully aware of all the things that could happen, Wyatt. That's why I wanted to handle this myself. I didn't want anyone else getting involved. The more people who are involved, the higher the chances of everything going haywire."

"That's ridiculous, Colter."

"No, it's not. The last thing this ranch needs is more drama. Mom and Dad are already struggling to make ends meet. Don't you realize that everything is at stake?" He slid the board into place as Wyatt moved toward him.

Wyatt squatted down and held the board in place. "Are they really that bad off?"

Colter nodded. "If this stuff gets out, it'll only get worse. I didn't want to risk it." He screwed the board into place. "As long as we work together, you and I—and this place—we got a chance. United we stand…"

"Divided we fall," Wyatt said, finishing his sentence.

There was the sound of the barn door opening, and they fell silent. Colter looked over the edge of the loft. Standing just inside the door, looking as though she wanted to be anywhere else but there, was Whitney. She looked up at him, her hand still on the barn's door.

Wyatt looked over the edge and forced a smile. "Heya, Whitney. How's it going?"

"Hey," she said, with a little wave. "I saw your car outside. What's going on?" She frowned up at him.

She must have been upset still, rightly, but Colter didn't want to talk about it in front of his brother. Knowing Wyatt, he would point fingers at her as a suspect—right now he'd be looking at everyone with that cynical scrutiny of his. Whitney didn't deserve that kind of thing. She'd already been through so much, and in his gut Colter just knew that, regardless of what Sarah had accused her of, she wasn't capable of that kind of evil.

Wyatt leaned over. "Does she know everything?" he whispered.

Colter nodded. "We found more, Whit. Someone has been up in the loft and making more of the Molotov cocktails."

"Is that why you called your brother here? You think I have something to do with it?" Whitney asked, wringing her hands nervously.

"What?" Colter asked, confused.

"You know, after what Sarah told you. You don't think I'd really do something like that, do you?" Her voice was strained, making her sound as though she was on the verge of tears. "I promise... I don't know where she heard something so stupid, but I loved Rudy. I loved...I loved it all... I love that world. I miss it so much." She covered her face, masking her tears as they fell.

Colter climbed down the ladder and walked over to her, taking her into his arms. Wyatt and his opinions be damned. "You're okay. I know you. I know you wouldn't do something that heinous. She's just jealous and upset."

She shook in his arms as she sobbed. "I thought that coming here... Everything would get easier. That I wouldn't have to face it every day... That I could start fresh."

"Shh... You don't need to cry. You are starting fresh. We're starting fresh. And more than anything, I want you to know that I trust you." He ran his hand over her hair, trying to soothe her. "You're okay."

Wyatt made his way down from the loft, and as he hung the hammer and saw on the wall behind the bench, he gave Colter a questioning look, but Colter wasn't sure if it was because of their relationship or the things that she was saying. Either way, he would have to answer a slew of questions when he and Wyatt were alone.

Whitney stepped out of his arms and moved backward toward the open barn door as though she suddenly had realized where she was standing. "I'm sorry, guys. I didn't mean to interrupt. It was just—"

"No worries," Wyatt said, waving her off. "I know how it can be. Gwen and I have been through a lot, too. Sometimes you just have to communicate. At least that's what she tells me," he said with a chuckle.

Whitney smiled, dabbing at her cheeks. "I'm not a crier, I promise."

"I know you're tough stuff. My mother wouldn't have just anybody working for her," Wyatt said, clearly trying to make her feel better.

He and Colter both knew only too well that their mother and father didn't always have the best judgment when it came to the hiring they did for the place. They always had a soft spot for sob stories and hard-up cases, but Colter appreciated his brother's gesture to make her feel better.

Whitney looked over at him, and he could see that she was thinking the same thing.

"Thinking about Mom and Dad," Wyatt continued, "do you think that we should tell them anything?"

Colter shook his head. "I think we could tell Dad, but he'd tell Mom. Let's just wait until Yule Night is over. In the meantime, is there anything you can pull from the bottles? Fingerprints or anything?"

Wyatt nodded. "We could, but that would involve getting my department in on this. And if they think we should get the ATF or FBI out here… Well, that's a whole can of worms that I don't want to open." He ran his hands over his face. "Maybe keeping me in the dark on this one wasn't such a bad idea. I can't *not* investigate this, Colter."

"Thanks for finally seeing things from my perspective, man," Colter said with a chuckle. "You need to give us a few days, at least until after the party, before we start getting other people involved. Hopefully by then, this will all have stopped or we will have the person responsible in custody."

"We're going to have to work fast," Wyatt said. "Do you guys have any idea, any clues as to who may be behind this?"

Colter shrugged, but Whitney glanced outside.

"Whitney?" Wyatt asked as he must have noticed her reaction.

She nibbled at her lip. "I…I just have a feeling that Sarah is involved. Whoever is doing this has to know something about how the ranch functions. She has been around a lot lately."

"Why would she do something like that? And threaten everyone?" Wyatt asked.

She looked over at Colter and then down at the floor.

"Let's just say that Sarah has some misplaced feelings when it comes to me," Colter said, trying to take some of the pressure off her.

Wyatt gave him a knowing look. "So she's a jilted lover?"

Colter almost choked and had to cough to clear the distaste from his mouth. "No. We're not lovers. We went out once, but it was nothing like that. But, even so, I don't think she would stoop to hurting or threatening anyone on the ranch. She made a point of telling me that her success depends on the ranch's success. I just don't think she has it in her. She may be imperfect, but she's not evil—not like that."

"You found this all out when you *went out with her*?" Whitney asked, shock infusing her words.

"It was right after her divorce. We were set up, and it didn't go well. Seriously, it was bad. I think that's why she wants another shot to make things better this time."

Wyatt shifted his weight, clearly uncomfortable with what was happening in front of him. "I'm going to step out back," he said, walking over to the side door of the barn. "When you're done…" He clicked the door shut behind him.

Colter tried to ignore the tangle of nerves that had descended on him. The last thing he wanted to do right now was fight with Whitney. He had been hoping that they could just move forward, that everything could just be forgiven and forgotten, yet when emotions got involved, it always seemed to go awry.

He turned to face Whitney, and as he opened his mouth to try to reassure her, she came rushing toward him, flinging her arms around him. She crushed her mouth to his. She ran her tongue over the bottom of his lip, sucking and pulling it between her teeth. It felt so good, soft and warm, yet flecked with the scraping of her teeth against him. It was everything great about a kiss—promises of more, heat and passion, yet the dangerous hints of the kinds of pains that always came with ecstasy. He loved everything about it—and her for it.

He pressed her against the wall of the barn and lifted her hands above her, holding them with one hand as the other searched for her skin beneath her winter coat. He slid his hand up, unquestioning, unwavering in his need to feel her. He pushed his hands under the edges of her bra and cupped her soft skin. She was so warm, but as he ran his finger over her nipples, they pressed against him like perfect little nubs. He wished he could lift her shirt and pull them into his mouth. He wanted to taste her so badly that he moaned.

She sucked in her breath, and the cold air glazed over the place on his lips made warm by her kiss. God, she could do things to him that made him long for her like he had never longed for anyone before. He wanted to take her, here, now, hard.

There was the creak of the side door. "Guys, you have to take a look—" Wyatt stopped and cleared his throat.

Colter slipped his hand out from under her jacket, and taking a moment to collect himself, he turned to face his brother. "What is it?"

"I, uh, think I found something," Wyatt said, but he stared at the ground as Whitney readjusted her shirt and jacket.

Colter tried not to feel sorry for himself as they made their way out of the barn, following his brother. It always seemed that as soon as something started going right, the world had a terrible habit of getting in the way.

He slipped his hand in Whitney's. If nothing else, at least she had seemed to forgive him and maybe had implied that they could really, truly start fresh. He'd take her kiss as a good sign.

"Look," Wyatt said, stopping near the side of the barn and pointing at a set of tire tracks in the fresh snow. "Do you notice anything strange about them?"

Colter shook his head. They looked like regular tire tracks, but then again, he wasn't trained in forensics.

"Look right there," Wyatt said, squatting down and pointing at the pattern. It was deep and made up of a pattern of triangles and ridges. "That right there is a new set of tires. Look at the tread. And based on the pattern, it's not just any set of tires, but BF Goodrich All-Terrains."

"What does that mean?" Whitney asked.

Wyatt smiled. It was the smile of a man who knew exactly what he was doing. It was the smile of a man who was about to win. "Those tires are expensive truck tires. Tires we don't use on any of the ranch vehicles."

"How do you know that this person was the one going into the barn to make explosives?" Colter asked.

"There was only one set of footprints when I came out here. They were leading to and from the side door of the barn, but nowhere else." He motioned around them. "And whoever parked here must have realized that their truck couldn't be seen by anyone unless they were out in the pasture areas. It's a great place to park if you don't want to be caught."

"That's all circumstantial," Colter said, feeling like he was raining on his brother's attempt to help.

Wyatt's smile widened. "Sure… All except that." He motioned over to the snow where there was a single beer cap lying only slightly sunken into the snow, almost as though it had simply fallen out of someone's hand. On the cap was the distinctive red star of those that had been in the loft.

"Who do you know that drives a truck?" Wyatt continued. "Someone who has the money to drop into high-end tires? If you can figure that out, I think we may have just found our man."

Chapter Fifteen

No matter what Sarah said, she had to be behind it. Whitney checked all the boxes. Motivation. Opportunity. New truck. Money. Whether or not Colter wanted to see the woman for who she really was and what she was capable of was up to him, but Whitney wasn't falling for the woman's games. She knew all too well how spurned lovers could do things that would surprise a person—and how little they cared about the truth or the cost their actions would have on others. All they saw was the person they loved and nothing else—it was what made them so dangerous, their lack of empathy and their disregard for consequences.

The thought made shivers run through her.

Maybe someday the ghosts of her past would leave her, but hoping for something so unrealistic seemed like an exercise in futility.

Colter and Wyatt were taking pictures of the tire tracks. She felt bad for the brothers, who were both in a terrible predicament. It was hard to be in a place where you couldn't tell the truth out of fear it would affect the lives around you. She'd been there too many times. She thought back to when she had first realized that Frank was stalking her. It had been at the prom. She'd gone out with her friends and a boy whom she had known since grade school. The boy was gay but hadn't told anyone except her.

When they were at dinner, Frank had looked in the window of the restaurant. Even without closing her eyes, she could still see him standing there, his warm breath fogging up the glass as he stared daggers at her date's back. When they came out of the restaurant, her date's car's tires had been slashed and they'd had to call her mother and father to take them to the high school for the party. They hadn't done much dancing. Her date had been consumed with trying to find a way to get his tires replaced and all she had been able to think about was whether or not she should tell anyone.

In the end, she hadn't turned Frank in out of fear that he would strike again. She had tried to explain to him that her date was nothing but a friend when he threatened to come after him. Luckily, when she'd told him about his sexual orientation, it made things easier and he'd promised to lay off. Yet nothing about it had made her feel good. She had felt completely bound to the will of a madman. He had seemed unstoppable and capable of anything. And, if anything, her terror of him and what he was willing to do to hurt her had been well-founded.

She had made so many mistakes in her past. She couldn't allow herself to make another in her present. Making her way to the parking lot, she noticed that Sarah's truck was missing. Strange. Maybe the woman had seen them go into the barn, or overheard them and had hightailed it out of there before she could fall under suspicion.

Too late.

Whitney looked down at her watch. If she rushed into town she would still have time to do what needed to be done. For a moment she thought about going back to tell Wyatt and Colter where she was going and what she was thinking, but Colter would just come to Sarah's aid. It was what he always did; he couldn't be objective. As much as it should have annoyed her, that he would still have a soft spot for his former girlfriend—or whatever he would have classified her as—it didn't. His graciousness of spirit was something that she admired about him.

He had been through just as much as she had, yet he wasn't hardened by the world. Instead he always seemed to take it in stride and deal with things as they came to him without looking at all the pain and memories.

If only she could be more like him, and was able to learn to forgive and live for the present instead of being held back by the weight of her past.

It didn't take long to grab the keys and hit the road. She passed by Colter's truck as she made her way carefully down the road and to town. By the time she made it to Sarah's shop, dusk had started to descend on the little town and its late-nineteenth-century-style buildings. The town was quaint and full of charm, a throwback to an era and a lifestyle that was completely different from now. She wondered what it would have been like to live in a time like that, when the West was still wild, lives revolved around mining and stripping away minerals and oil from the lands, a world where danger lurked around every corner.

Thinking about it, she wondered if maybe it wasn't really so different from life now. Only the clothes and manners in which they went about mining had changed. In Kentucky, coal was their main source of mineral wealth rather than gold, silver and uranium. There, when she'd been growing up, the old-time miners had still been succumbing to black lung, while in Montana the workers were falling to a variety of cancers caused by the chemicals used in mining.

No doubt, in twenty years another generation of miners would succumb to some mysterious disease brought on by their livelihoods and the swords they had chosen to live by.

She got out of the truck. Since she had left the ranch and the sun had gone down, the temperature had fallen at least twenty degrees and the cold had taken on the same dangerous edge as the night before. As she thought about the hike and being stuck out in the cold with Colter, a certain warmth took hold in her belly. Even though it was a terrible situation, she wouldn't have wanted to take it all back. It was one heck of an adventure; and life should be spent in adventures—the kind that made her want to hold her breath, the kind that made her heart hurt from happiness and joy, and the kind that could be shared with those she truly cared about.

Whether or not the time was right, or that it was a good decision, Colter was the man she wanted in her life. She couldn't justify giving her heart away in any logical way, but there was something about him that made her thankful that she had come to this place, where life still spoke to bygone eras and intrigue. She loved this place almost as much as she loved him.

Making her way to the front door of the café, she stopped and stared inside. The place looked warm, and bits of condensation had started to collect at the corners of the front bay windows and frieze. It made the mural look as though it was painted on a layer of ice. Sarah was nowhere to be seen, but there was some metallic banging that sounded like pans coming from inside the kitchen.

She had no idea what she was going to say to the woman, or the kinds of questions she should ask.

A part of her wondered if she was even on the right track, or if she was a bit like Colter and unable to be objective because of the way she felt about the woman. She hated the thought that perhaps she was falsely accusing Sarah—she had been in those shoes, but the one doing the finger-pointing was the same woman in question. There was nothing like a little projection—when the guilty person was caught, he always had a way of pointing the finger away from himself.

Perhaps more than anything, what she feared if she was wrong was the fact that the guilt might fall to someone else whom she knew far better and who scared her far worse—Frank.

Just the thought of his being there made her stomach ache and a wave of nausea pass over her. She hated that the thought of him could still provoke a physical response. She hated that he still held the power of terror over her. It was so wrong. Yet there was no making it right. All she could do was hope that he hadn't found out where she was, and that he wasn't behind this.

Heck, if he was, it would be just like he had been a few years ago when he stuck his face in the window of the restaurant and ruined her night. He'd never been particularly sneaky when it came to her. If anything, he'd only been good at not getting caught—or at least penalized for his crimes.

She looked back over her shoulder thanks to the thoughts of Frank. He wasn't there; he couldn't be—unless that was who Sarah had been talking to. It would have made sense. He had always accused her of setting that fire—even in court he had told his lawyer that she was responsible for it. He was the king of gaslighting—so good, in fact, that his lawyer had ultimately taken his side and believed his lies and tried hard to prove that his client wasn't guilty. He had nearly gotten him acquitted.

No one was on the sidewalks. Most of the stores were still open, but this was likely out of some desperate hope that people would come in for their Christmas shopping. There were a few cars parked along the road, but none she recognized.

She slipped into the café. The place always smelled so good, like warm bread and butter, but today it had something different in the air—almost musky like some kind of spice used in antiquity. She tried to put her finger on the smoky scent, but try as she might, it wouldn't come to her.

"Sarah?" she called, hoping that she would just think of the right thing to say the moment the woman came out of the kitchen.

There was no answer.

"Hello? Is anyone here?" she asked, walking toward the back and the kitchen, where she had met Sarah's cousins. There was the sound of glass breaking and she rushed toward the noise.

As she dashed into the kitchen, the back door slammed shut. Someone in a dark brown knit cap and heavy work coat sprinted to the left and out of sight.

"Wait!" she screamed. "Stop!"

She moved to go after the person, but was stopped by the heat. On the floor, and running up the wall, was a fire. Terror filled her. All she could do was stare at the blue base and orange curling tips of the flame.

There was liquid. Accelerant. She had seen it before. She had felt the heat. The same heat.

She was going to die. This was the end. There was no way she could make it out of a fire again. Her luck was gone. This was the way she was meant to go.

She could be with Rudy.

Black smoke poured up from the flames, filling the kitchen with its spicy, acrid stench—the scent of burning motor oil and gas. Oh, God, she hated that smell.

She had to move. She couldn't just stand here and let it have her.

Fight. She had to fight.

This time, there was no one to save—only herself— she had to make the choice. She couldn't stay here.

Forcing herself to look away from the fire, she broke the spell it had cast upon her.

She ran toward the front door. There, the window that had only minutes before been covered in ice was now shattered on the floor like spent tears. At the center was a steadily growing circle of fire around a green Heineken bottle that thankfully hadn't been broken when it was thrown through the glass.

Someone had tried to trap her.

They *had* trapped her.

She looked through the flames toward the door. She'd have to move quick to get out. The only way out was around the side of the room that was steadily filling with the black smoke.

The smoke. It always got a victim first.

She got down on her knees and started moving toward the wall and around the steadily growing pool of flames. The broken glass on the floor cut at her hands and pierced through her jeans and pressed into her knees, but she didn't care. She simply kept moving forward. Another foot. Just one more foot. One more.

Finally, she found the door and pressed out into the night. As she spilled out on the steps and down to the sidewalk, she saw the reflection of red and blue lights coming from the distance. She closed her eyes and let her body fall into the snow and ice that littered the sidewalk.

She had fought—and once again, she'd won. She'd survived.

Chapter Sixteen

Colter's buddies had called him the moment they saw the ranch truck outside the café, but they hadn't needed to—he and Wyatt had heard the call on his radio while they were pulling his truck out of the snowbank.

He should have known where Whitney had gone. One minute she was with them, talking about the tire tracks, and the next she had disappeared. Just when he thought he knew the girl, she did something like this.

All he could hope was that she was really okay. His friend had said she had gotten out in time, just some smoke inhalation, but she would be fine. Though Colter knew his friend had been telling him the truth, his heart wouldn't let him believe it until he saw her with his own two eyes.

He pulled the truck to a stop and got out. The building was engulfed in flames, and the fire crew was doing its best to stop the fire's advancement into nearby buildings. These old places were built with brick and mortar, but they had enough wood in them that one bad fire could easily jump to the next building if they didn't get on top of it quickly.

Whitney wasn't anywhere to be seen. Where was she?

The battalion chief, his friend Turner, was standing next to the crew, giving an order to one of the men on the hose. Colter made his way over to them as the BC turned toward him.

"Why aren't you in your gear?" Turner asked, from his tone only half kidding. "We could use an extra set of hands."

"I was at the ranch, but if you want, I can—"

Turner waved him off. "We're hoping to get another truck in here from rural. We'll see how quick they get here."

They were in dire straits if they were calling in reinforcements from the volunteer rural sector. Colter should have been working, but he couldn't go get his gear and get back here—at least not until he found Whitney.

He glanced around, but couldn't see her. However, across the street was Sarah's black Chevy pickup.

There was a collection of people who had spilled out from the stores on Main Street and the nearby homes, no doubt all come to see the biggest source of gossip this week. This would at least keep them from talking about his family for a little bit, though... He was sure they would be tied back to this.

He stopped. What if this fire did have something to do with his family and the threat they had received?

"Was there anyone else in the building at the time of the fire besides Whitney?" Colter asked.

"I don't know. Ms. Barstow hasn't spoken to anyone." Turner shrugged. "She's with the EMTs now."

Colter turned to leave, heading in the direction of the lights of the ambulance.

"Wait," Turner said, grabbing him by the arm to stop him. "How well do you know this girl?" There was a look of deep concern in his eyes.

"Pretty well. Why?" Colter hated the way his friend was looking at him. It was like there was something more, something he was afraid to ask or tell him. "What are you thinking, Turner?"

He let go of his arm. "This fire was no accident." He skidded his bunker boot around in the slushy, wet snow. "Sarah made a point of telling me that there had been some kind of incident between her and your friend. She seems to be of the mind that Whitney had something to do with this thing. And you know, if that's the case…"

He didn't have to say anything more.

"Whitney wouldn't do this. She's innocent," Colter said, meaning it with every ounce of his being. Yet, as he said it, a nagging feeling rose from his gut.

What if he was wrong? What if he'd been wrong about this woman all along?

No. He trusted her. She had revealed her past to him. She had told him about her past, and the pain that came with it. And her opening up like that, trusting him, was a gift. If he listened to the idle gossip and naysayers around him, what kind of person would he be? He needed to respect and appreciate her, and trust her for the person he knew her to be, not the person others were portraying her as. In the long run, the truth would come to light—he would look back on this and either be humbled or be proud of his actions.

Today, he would stand up for what he knew was right and for the love he held in his heart.

Today, he would fight for her.

"Colter, how can you be sure she's not behind this?" Turner continued. "From what Sarah had to say, this girl has only been around for a couple of months. You notice that as soon as she started working here, trouble has been cropping up regularly."

"You know just as well as I do she's not responsible for everything at the ranch."

He tried to stanch the anger that was boiling up inside him. Turner didn't mean anything by it, and he couldn't possibly know how Colter felt about her. If anything, he was just trying to make sure he was doing his job, but it didn't make the contempt Colter was feeling for his friend any easier to bear.

"The last thing this girl would do is have anything to do with another fire. She is terrified of the damn thing. This just isn't something she's capable of. Trust me."

Turner's eyebrows rose and his eyes darkened. "What do you mean *another fire*? Is there something

I need to know about? Something that pertains to this case that you aren't telling me, Colter?"

He shook his head, wishing that he hadn't opened his stupid mouth.

"If you don't talk to me, Colter, you will find yourself in need of another job." Whatever friendship they had seemed to fall apart with his words.

"You don't have the power to fire me, Turner."

"If you are withholding information that will tell me who is behind this fire, then you can make damn sure that this will find its way to the powers that be, who will gladly throw you out on your ass."

Colter raised his hands in submission. This was going in a direction he couldn't let it go. He couldn't risk everything just because he was pissed and felt like he needed to protect her. "Look, Turner, you and I are friends," he started. "Let's not blow this all out of proportion."

"Then answer my question, Fitzgerald," Turner said through gritted teeth.

He sighed. "Whitney and her family were victims of an arson a while back. It's why she's here. She's running from her past."

Turner nodded, listening.

"You just have to believe me when I say that I don't think she's behind this," Colter continued. "If she is, I'll..."

"You'll what?" Turner asked, this time some of the anger seeming to seep from his tone.

"I'll throw in my hat. No investigation. No fight. I'll just quit."

Turner nodded, apparently mollified. "Okay. I'll have my guy look elsewhere, but you better hope to all that is holy that you aren't wrong and love ain't blind."

Colter turned around and made his way toward the ambulance in hopes Turner couldn't see the look of complete shock over what he had just agreed to that he was sure was on his face. He had just gambled his entire future on a feeling.

Colter was a lot of things, but he had never thought himself a fool. It wasn't time to start changing his feelings toward himself now. He'd just have to ride it out and pray he had been right.

But he'd been wrong before.

He'd never thought his biological parents would have been the kind to leave him. Sure, he'd been a kid and naive, but he had trusted them—and they had done him wrong. And here he was, back in the same position of blindly trusting someone he loved.

The back doors of the ambulance were closed and he knocked on them before opening. Whitney was sitting on the gurney, alone. An oxygen mask was over her soot-covered face, but even under the ash he could tell she was pale. The look in her eyes told him that she'd been to hell and back.

He stepped up into the back of the ambulance and, careful not to touch her in case she was hurt, sat down next to her. "Are you okay?"

She wrung her hands and looked down at her fingers. They were covered in black ash, and her nail beds were as pale as her face. If he wasn't careful, she could easily slip into shock. He had to get her talking. Anything would be fine as long as it took her mind off what had just happened.

"Lassie wants you to come home," he said, trying his very best to make her laugh.

She blinked a few times but remained silent and staring.

"You should have seen the little rat dog. She's been running in circles trying to tell me something. If I was smart, I would have known that she was trying to warn me. You'd think I'd speak dog by now."

She looked up, and her lips trembled as though she wanted to smile. She pulled the oxygen mask from her face, letting it drop to her neck. "You're certainly fluent in smart-ass."

He laughed, but the boom made her twitch and he shut up.

"We all have gifts. And really, I think my articulateness is really due to my brothers. They trained me so I could bring my very best to the dating table." He leaned closer and brushed back her hair, thankful when she didn't shudder from his fingers grazing against her skin. "I mean, it got you. Didn't it?"

"Colter..."

The way she said his name told him that he wasn't going to like whatever was going to come next.

"Stop," he said, cutting her off before she could go

any further. "I'm a real catch. I mean, who wouldn't want all this?" He raised his arms, flexing them like some kind of bodybuilder on display.

"You really are ridiculous," she said with a little giggle.

"Oh, baby, you ain't seen nothin' yet," he said, some of the trepidation he'd been feeling disappearing with the sound of her laugh. "If the goon squad says you can, how about we get out of here?"

"They want my statement," she said, and some of the color that had finally come back to her cheeks disappeared.

"They can wait until tomorrow. I'll just tell them that they can stop by the ranch. Sound good?"

She nodded and her lips turned up into a slight, relieved smile.

"I'll be right back." He slipped out and walked up to Turner.

It didn't take long for him to get the man to agree to let them head back to the ranch, but it had come with another stern reminder of what hung in the balance.

Chapter Seventeen

The ride back to the ranch seemed to take longer than usual, but it could have rested in the fact that he had made sure to drive extra slow in an effort to keep his truck on the road. They couldn't go on a hike through the tundra as they had the night before. Not that he had minded spending more time with her. It was just that he hated the fact that he had put her in needless danger.

Nothing seemed to go right when it came to their time together.

He put his hand in the middle and she slipped her fingers into his, not saying a word. For a thousand reasons, most of which she had been careful to express to him, they couldn't be together and he heard them all—but there was no stopping what the heart wanted.

"Do you want to tell me what happened in there?" He ran his thumb over hers.

She sighed and stared out into the night. "I don't want to talk about it. I never want to talk about it…"

He could understand her response, but part of him had to know what had gone down.

"I covered for you back there," he said. "They seemed to think that the fire was suspicious. They wanted to take you in, but I held them off."

She finally looked over at him and she gave his hand a squeeze. "You did that for me?"

He nodded.

"Why?"

His gut ached as he thought of the risk he had taken. "I know you. I know what a good person you are. If I thought for a second that you actually had anything to do with it, we wouldn't be here right now—we wouldn't have ended up where we were last night, either. Kissing, I mean."

"Do you really think you know me?"

The ache intensified. "I think I do. Do you think you know me?"

She smiled. "Your favorite food is ham, potato casserole and green beans. And you love action movies."

He laughed. "How do you know that?"

"Your mother was talking about it. She said you're an avid *Lethal Weapon* fan."

"You were talking to my mother about me?" He was equally surprised and pleased. "So, how long have you been in love with me?"

"Shut up." She clenched his hand. "You know how I feel."

Right now he wasn't entirely sure. He understood

what she was implying and what she had told him she
wanted and how she felt, but when they were together
there was just something magical between them.

He pulled the truck to a stop as they got to the
ranch. It had been his plan to go home tonight and
finally get into his own bed instead of staying at his
parents', but right now the last thing he wanted was
his own pillow.

She wouldn't want to have anything to happen
between them. Not after everything.

He got out of the truck and walked over to her
side. He was overthinking this. There was no point
fretting about any of it. Regardless of how confused he was, she had made her wishes clear—they
couldn't be together.

That didn't mean that he couldn't be a gentleman
and see her to her door.

She stepped out of the truck and took his hand.
She gave it a squeeze but said nothing and led him
to the house.

The place was quiet, though it wasn't particularly
late—at least not in comparison to last night.

She walked into her bedroom. It was small, maybe
a bit cramped.

When he'd been a kid her bedroom was kept as a
place for guests to stay. Thinking about it, he wondered why his mother had put her there. Had she not
assumed that Whitney would stay?

He pushed the thoughts from his mind. His mother

had a method to everything she did, and he wasn't about to start questioning it now.

Colter stopped at the door and let go of Whitney's hand, letting it slip from his fingers like hopes. "Have a good night. If you need anything, I can stay or… I was going to head home." He motioned toward the hall, fully aware of how awkward it was between them.

He wanted to follow her into her room, push her down onto the bed, but he couldn't. Not now and, for all he knew, not ever.

"Do you really want to go home?" she asked, a hint of longing in her voice.

Or maybe it wasn't longing but his need to hear a longing that he heard.

"I…I don't have to. I can sleep out on the couch or something." He looked down the long, empty hall-way.

"There was someone in Sarah's café… Tonight," she said, catching him off guard.

"What? Who? You *saw* someone?"

She took his hand and closed the door. She pulled out the chair at her tiny desk and motioned for him to sit down. "I don't know if it was a man or a woman. I just saw someone running out after they threw the bottle."

"They threw a bottle? Why didn't you tell anyone what you saw?"

She shrugged. "I was shaken up. And I didn't

know what you had said and to whom. I wanted to make sure I didn't get you into trouble."

He stepped closer to her, taking in the scent of smoke from her skin and the heat of her nearness. Ever so carefully, he reached up and cupped her face in his hands. "You don't need to worry about me. You never have to worry about me. I will handle whatever needs to be handled, but you need to keep yourself safe and out of trouble. If they knew you were hiding something like that… I told you that they thought—"

She touched her finger to his lips, stopping him from going into a full tirade. "I'll talk to them in the morning. Everything will be okay."

She traced her finger around his lips, making his body come to life.

"In the meantime," she whispered as she leaned toward him and pulled away her finger before her lips met his. "I need to forget, and I want to explore."

HIS LIPS WERE slightly chapped, the mark of cold winter weather and the dry air of Montana. She moved to her tiptoes, and his breath caressed her lips as she drew nearer to him. There were still millimeters between them, yet this was the closest emotionally she had been to anyone in a long time—ever since Frank. Not that she wanted to think about Frank. Not now. Not ever. But with the fire…it was no wonder she had gone back to that place and time. No matter how hard she fought against the memories of him, his actions would always leave a mark on the canvas of her life.

She leaned back slightly as thoughts of him moved through her.

Maybe it was a mistake, taking this step with Colter. Anytime she grew close to a man, it was only bound to end in agony. Colter was a good man, an everyday hero, but that didn't guarantee that things between them would end in anything but heartbreak. If truth be told, she wasn't sure her heart would stand being broken again—but she couldn't keep on a path that meant she stopped living. She needed this. She needed him.

She needed a future that brought happiness. And right now the happiness and escape she longed for could only be found in his kiss.

"Are you okay?" he asked, his voice airy and light as his thumbs moved over her cheeks.

She reached up and took his hand in hers. "I'm going to be fine as long as you kiss me."

It was exactly the invitation he needed. He rushed to her lips, the coarse lines of his pressing against hers, a harsh comparison to her softness, but she liked the way they scratched against hers. It was almost as if his lips were pulling her closer, reaching for more.

He ran his tongue over the places where his lips had rubbed, and the sensation made her think of all the places his tongue could travel on her body. She ached for more. So much more. She reached up and ran her fingers through his short hair. It was soft but sharp from a fresh cut—just like the rest of him, it was the perfect combination. Perhaps he was made to be the man she had always been longing for.

His kiss moved from her lips and over her neck. She let her head fall back, reveling in the touch of him against the tender lines of her collarbone. As he kissed, he moved her toward the bed, and as her legs touched it, he picked her up and wrapped her legs around his waist. She could feel his responding body rubbing against her, telling her that he wanted this just as much as she did.

He laid her down on the bed, their bodies flexing and pushing against each other. In one fluid motion, he reached down and opened the buttons of her shirt, revealing her lace bra. As he sat up and pulled the shirt from her, she caught the scent of smoke and lust. It was a heady mix, danger and want—the scent of love.

"Dance for me," she said, trying to get back control over the urgency that she had been feeling. She wanted to savor their time together—every second of it.

"What?" he asked with a surprised laugh. "Really?"

"Or I could dance for you," she offered with a playful tip of her head.

"You…always surprise me." He stood up and gave her a sexy, almost shy grin.

He started to hum as he pulled up the edge of his shirt. It wasn't a song that she recognized, but it sounded a bit like an old country hit. He swiveled his hips as his fingers moved down the buttons of his shirt. Slipping the last button free, he turned around and gave her a playful wiggle of his behind.

She laughed. "Oh, yeah, baby. Just like that."

He gave his butt a playful slap as he started to get into it, moving and dancing as he unbuckled his pants.

He really did have a nice ass. Unable to control herself, she reached up and gave it a little squeeze. It was just as muscular as the rest of him.

"Hey, now, no touching the merchandise," he said, pulling out of her grasp.

"But what if I want to touch you?" she asked with a little whine.

He gave her a lift of his brow. "How bad do you want it?"

She wiggled her finger, motioning for him. "Come here and I'll show you."

He took a step.

She reached up and took hold of the waist of his jeans and pulled him even closer. His body was pumping off heat. The palm of her hand moved against him as she lowered his zipper, exposing his red-and-black gingham boxers. She let his pants drop to the floor and he stepped out of them.

"Very classy," she said, tugging at the bottom of the leg of his boxers. It wasn't that they were anything remarkable, but sitting there alone in her room with him, she suddenly felt the reality of the entire situation—and what it would mean.

If she went there with him, everything would change. There would be no going back to being simple friends. Even if they did this only once, the air between them would always be flecked with the knowledge that they had spent this night together. He would know her as very few men did, and she would know him.

The act of lovemaking was a gift, and once given, the memory of those moments spent together would last a lifetime. There was no forgetting the way a man felt in her arms, or the way his kiss moved over her lips. There was no ignoring the little jolt of excitement she would feel whenever he was near.

She wanted it all.

Reaching down, she slipped off her jeans and her panties. He sucked in a breath as he watched her shimmy them off and drop them to the floor atop his pants.

"You are so beautiful."

She moved to cover her nakedness, to make up for her mistake with the convenience store's camera in some way, but she stopped herself. Men wanted a woman who was confident, who took control in the bedroom and wasn't afraid to be who she was. She hadn't been that woman in the past, but she had been through so much. The one thing she could give to herself was love and acceptance, the same things she wanted from him.

Instead of covering her breasts, she ran her fingers over her curves and smiled up at him. She lay down on the edge of the bed, her hair splaying around her. With her feet, she reached up and pulled down his boxers.

He was the perfect man, and as thick and proportionate as the rest of him.

"Come here," she whispered, running her fingers down her belly, teasing him as she brushed against the soft tuft of hair between her legs.

He moaned as he stepped closer. He leaned in and kissed the inside of her knee. Each kiss moved incrementally higher until she met his mouth. It felt so good, his tongue against her, that she could barely breathe.

"I…want…you…" she said, running her fingers through his hair.

He looked up at her.

"Please," she begged.

He smiled and moved until he was pressed against her. He kissed her lips and thrust into her, making her call out his name with ecstasy.

Their bodies did all the talking that was required. It was more than she had expected, or ever could have imagined—feeling him inside her.

There was no doubt—he had been meant for her.

Chapter Eighteen

If Colter could have asked for one thing for Christmas, it was that he would have a lifetime of what he'd had last night. Whitney Barstow was nothing short of amazing. It wasn't just the sex that had him thinking of only her this morning as he puttered around the ranch, cleaning out the stalls and getting the barn ready for tonight's Yule Night festivities.

Sure, the sex had been great, but there was so much more to it and the way he was feeling about her. He couldn't even really remember what his life had been like before her, as she seemed to fill him up. Every time he closed his eyes, all he could see was her smile and the way her hair had haloed around her head on her pillow when he forced himself to get out of bed.

He hadn't wanted to leave, but he had thought it better that way—he didn't want anyone at the ranch to know their private life and about the moments they shared.

Though he knew they wouldn't be able to keep their blooming relationship secret for long, he had to honor her request for utmost privacy—though he wanted to shout her name from the top of the grain silos for the whole world to hear and to know that she was his entire world.

He raked the hay as he was met with the telltale sound of the grinding metal as the barn door opened.

"Hello?" he asked, unintentionally sounding annoyed at the prospect of someone disturbing the thoughts he was having of last night and being in Whitney's arms.

"Colter?" Whitney called. "Are you in here?"

He dumped his rake and poked his head out of the stall. "I'm in here. How'd you sleep?"

She left the door open, looking at it one more time before making her way toward him. "It was just fine until I woke up to find that you were gone. Did I do something wrong?"

It hadn't even occurred to him that she would have thought something like that after everything that had passed between them.

"Absolutely not. Are you crazy?" he said, wiping the thin sheen of sweat from his forehead with the back of his hand. "I just didn't want anyone to find out that…you know." He walked over to her and kissed her on the head. "You could never do anything wrong. At least not in bed. You were incredible."

She looked up at him and smiled. "I think you did the lion's share. Tonight I want to have a chance to take the reins."

He smiled wildly at her open invitation to once

again share her bed. "I'm pretty sure you took the reins several times last night, but I'm more than happy to let you do as you wish to my body." He laughed.

There was a light cough from the open door of the barn. His mother was standing in the open doorway, the snow behind her making her look like nothing more than a silhouette.

"Hey, Mom. Good morning," he said, stepping back from Whitney. His face warmed as he realized what his mother might have just heard him say.

"Mornin'," she said, coming in and starting to close the door behind her.

Whitney's eyes opened wide with fear as she watched Eloise.

"Mom, you mind leaving that open?" he asked, motioning for her to stop.

"Oh, yeah," she said, glancing toward Whitney with an apologetic tip of her head. "I forget, my dear. My apologies."

Whitney waved it off. "It's okay... It's getting better. It's just with last night...and the fire..."

"I completely understand. I was just being an old fool for forgetting," his mother said, moving toward them. "And actually, last night's fire was why I was coming to look for you. Wyatt told me everything about what you've found and the note. You shouldn't have kept it a secret."

"I was just trying to protect you."

"That's what Wyatt said, but you should know that I can handle the truth by now."

"I'm sorry. I thought you had enough on your plate."

She reached over and gave his hand a quick squeeze. "Have you talked to Sarah this morning?"

"No. Why?" Whitney did a good job of not letting her distaste for the other woman flicker over her face, though he was sure that she was thinking about her.

"I've been trying to reach her. She called and left a message that all the food for tonight's party was in the café. It's ruined." She sighed, but he could still see the stress and panic in her eyes. "I don't know what we're going to do. Who is going to want to come tonight when we don't have any food to give them? I wouldn't pay good money to come to a party only to be left hungry." She threw her hands up in the air with exasperation.

"Mom, no one is coming to Yule Night for the food. They come here to be with the people of the ranch, to celebrate."

She looked at him and gave him a weak smile. "That fire is going to be another mark against us. Whether we like it or not, people are talking about the fire and are starting to say that they think it had something to do with this ranch." She hugged her arms around herself and looked down at the concrete floor. "Maybe we should just cancel tonight. We can't risk the lives of our family, friends and guests just for some party."

"No," Whitney said, shaking her head as though by doing so she could stop his mother's words from filling her thoughts. "We can't let fear stop us from having the party—it has to go on. The ranch needs this source of income—"

"And we need to show the community that we're not going anywhere—that we're not afraid," Colter added.

"What if something does happen? What if everyone is right and whoever set the café on fire is just waiting for the right time? When everyone is in the barn? The last thing we need is another tragedy on our hands."

His mother was right. There could possibly be hundreds of people filling the barn and pouring out into the ranch's yards tonight. If someone wanted to send a horrendous message—tonight would be the night. They had been warned.

"What if we call in reinforcements?" he asked, smiling at his idea.

"Huh? What do you mean?" his mother asked.

"We could have Wyatt call a few of his department buddies, and I could call some of the guys from the station. I'm sure that they would all be happy to pitch in and help with security if we told them what was going on."

"You don't think they would try and stop tonight

from happening? You know, we don't want to put them at risk, too."

"First, we don't know for sure if that fire had anything to do with the ranch or the threats it has received." As he spoke, he knew how ridiculous that sounded. Of course the fire had something to do with the ranch and him—the green beer bottles and the fact that it happened the night before their party had to be more than coincidental. Whoever was after them was amping up their game.

Who knew what else they would be capable of? They were just lucky that no one had gotten hurt so far—though Whitney had come painfully close.

His mother gave him the look that told him that she had heard how ridiculous he had sounded, too.

"Okay, what if we do cancel it?" he asked. "What about the ranch?"

His mother's face pinched. "We've invested quite a bit into the party already, marketing, food, drink, invitations, deejay… The whole shebang, but it'll be okay."

"It won't be if you don't turn a profit from the event," Whitney said. "I saw the letter on your desk. You don't have to hide it."

"What were you doing looking at my private things?" His mother jumped and anger flashed over her features.

"I…I didn't mean to… I just meant…" Whitney stammered.

"Mom, she didn't mean to invade your privacy.

Besides, it's not as if we didn't know this place was going through a hard time."

Eloise's face fell and she sighed. "Of course. I'm sorry, Whitney. I didn't mean to get upset. It's just that…"

"You thought you could protect us," he said, reaching over and giving his mother's fingers a light squeeze. "And we love you for it, Mom. But for once, let us help you. Let's work together and do this for the place that we all love. We want this to be a success."

"What about the food?" she asked, not letting it go.

"Don't worry, Mom. I'm sure that we can figure something out. You just focus on getting everything lined up for tonight here."

His mother's eyes brimmed with unshed tears. "You really are a sweet boy. I'm so lucky to have you in my life." She threw her arms around his neck and gave him a quick kiss on the cheek before hurrying out of the barn.

His mother wasn't the kind who displayed much emotion. She was always metered in her approach and he could think of only a handful of times when he had seen her that close to tears. It only made him want to help her that much more.

Whitney turned to him. "What are we going to do?"

He waited until he couldn't see his mother. "I have no idea. Go to the store?"

"It would take hours to get everything we need and get back and put it all together," Whitney said, glancing down at her phone to check the time. "But I guess if we hurry, we can put something together."

"Are you a good cook?" he asked.

She gave him a guilty smile. "I can make grilled cheese sandwiches like nobody's business."

"And I can make peanut butter and jellies," he added.

Whitney laughed. "Okay, so cooking may not be our strong suit, but if it makes you feel any better, I can order takeout like nobody's business."

"I thought all Southern girls knew how to cook," he teased.

"And I thought all Northern boys knew how to mind their manners and be quiet," she said with a gentle, playful nudge.

"Whenever I'm with you, the last thing I want to do is be quiet." Before she could come up with a rebuttal, he pressed his lips against hers, hoping that it would make her think of last night and all the time they had shared making noise.

She pulled him closer, taking his lips with a hunger that made his thoughts race to the memory of her climbing on top of him. As hard as he tried, he couldn't stop his body from coming back to life and yearning for him to re-create last night.

She rubbed against him, teasing his body with the graze of her touch. "We have sandwiches to make," she said, pulling him back to some semblance of reality.

He groaned. She was right, but the last thing he wanted to do was go back to real life, where chores and danger waited.

Whitney stepped back from him and gave him a longing smile that told him that she wanted to continue things just as badly as he did.

A thought struck him. "You know who is a fantastic cook? Wyatt. I need to call him. Maybe he can help us out, too." He took out his phone, but before he dialed he took a few breaths and allowed his body to come back to normal.

"Even with him and Gwen, that is still going to be tough to get all the food bought, prepped and ready before the event. I mean, depending on what we end up doing, we may not even have enough oven space," Whitney said.

"I know, but if we don't have him help, we really will be stuck with sandwiches," he said, dialing his brother's number. "My mom and dad have been through enough. I want to make this special for them—something that they will never forget."

"I have a feeling, no matter what the food is—this is one Christmas that will be going down in their record books," she said with a sad smile.

"True, but I want it to be for something positive—not the year everything went to hell." He pressed the phone to his ear as it rang.

"Hey, brother, what's up?" Wyatt sounded tired and drawn.

"Did you guys find anything that could help us nail down the suspect?" Colter asked, hoping beyond all hopes that his brother would tell him that they had found the person responsible and that all his worries were for naught.

Wyatt sighed on the other end of the line. "Just some fragments of the bottles we were able to retrieve from the fire. Unfortunately, they weren't able to get any fingerprints. So I gave them some of the bottles we recovered from the barn. Same deal. It's almost as if whoever is behind this knew what our next play would be. They're brazen, but they're not entirely stupid.

"Did you come up with anything?" Wyatt asked.

Colter glanced over at Whitney and put his phone on mute. "I have to tell him about what you saw, or you do."

She nodded and motioned for the phone. Unmuting it, he handed it over.

"Hey, Wyatt, this is Whit. About last night…" She put it on speakerphone.

"What about it?"

Colter could hear the apprehension in his brother's tone.

"I saw someone as they were leaving. I didn't see their face, but from the body type, I think it was a man. He was wearing a dark brown knit hat and one of those buckskin-colored work jackets. You know, Carhartt or something."

"Why didn't you tell us about this last night?"

"I—"

"You can't be serious. You held back information that could have helped us figure out who this person is. The only real information we've gotten so far," Wyatt said, cutting her off in his rush to anger.

"Don't be upset with her, Wyatt. She thought she was doing the right thing," Colter said, trying to talk his brother down from the ledge.

"You two haven't done a single right thing over the last few days," Wyatt seethed. "I can't believe you. You should know better—and you should know what could be at stake by keeping something like this from me."

The world was pressing in on Colter from all directions. His brother wasn't wrong, but he didn't and couldn't possibly understand the kind of pressure and fear Whitney was feeling. All he seemed to see was the world from an officer's perspective—which was great, but also stopped him from feeling as Colter did.

"Whitney was upset. She's been through a lot. Cut her some slack."

There was a long pause on the other end of the line. Colter doubted his brother would step down; he wasn't the kind. With something like this he was like a dog with a bone—he wasn't going to let it go.

"Fine. I'll let the detective know about it. Is there

anything else you guys need to tell me—anything else you've been keeping a secret?" Wyatt pressed.

There were a lot of secrets floating around the place, but none he needed to know.

"We just talked to Mom. She's upset. All the food for tonight's party is gone."

Wyatt sucked in a long breath. "Does she have a plan?"

"She's totally overwhelmed. We managed to convince her not to cancel the party."

"Maybe that would have been for the best," Wyatt said.

"No. If they do, they'd lose thousands—and they needed to draw revenue from the event. Without it… I don't know what they're going to do."

"What do you need from me?" Wyatt said, not pressing the issue.

"First, we need to make sure that everyone here is going to stay safe. Do you think you can call some of your guys and have them come and keep a watch?" A truck rumbled to a stop in front of the barn, and from outside he could hear his mother talking to what sounded like a deliveryman.

"Done. I'll send a few down as soon as I can."

"Yeah," he said, looking out the window to see the florist's truck sitting in the parking lot. "There are going to be a lot of comings and goings today. If we could keep an eye on things, that would be great."

"About the food," Wyatt said. "I have an idea. You

guys don't worry about a thing. I have a few favors I think I could call in."

"What favors?"

"Don't worry about it. Just know that I've got it handled," Wyatt said, but some of the dryness had left his voice and he almost sounded excited.

It was in times like these, when the world was nothing more than a spinning ball of stress, that Colter loved being a part of this family. Though they had their problems and their histories, when push came to shove they all had each other's backs. Even more, they had been taught the art of forgiveness, understanding, the power and support that it meant to be a family, and above all—love.

Chapter Nineteen

As she laced a string of garland over the barn's door, Colter and his father set up the Christmas tree, and several of the staffers added lights and decorations to the barn. The place still carried the aroma of horses, but lingering over it was the scent of pine and the fresh cedar chips that they had put on the floor for the party. With each hour that passed, the place was starting to look more and more like something out of a Norman Rockwell painting and less like a place where disturbing events had occurred.

Colter and his family always left Whitney in awe. They weren't all biological family, yet they shared a bond and a love for each other that seemed to transcend any and all differences. She thought back to her own family. Not every Christmas was like this. There were the two years in which the holidays had ended in fights and turmoil between her boyfriend's family and her parents, and both had ended in tears.

She had always thought she'd had a good family, but watching this one made her realize that, while they were in the midst of turmoil, their true strength lay in their apparent ability to love each other—no matter what.

It was almost as if this family was the embodiment of what the Christmas spirit was meant to be. They were all selfless, protective, loving, caring and generous.

She loved Colter, but now seeing them together, she questioned her place in all of it. There was a part of her that made her wonder if she was good enough to fit into so much greatness. She had so many skeletons in her closet—and if Frank was behind this… As kind and affectionate as the family was, she wouldn't blame them if they didn't have the ability to forgive her for bringing that kind of turmoil into their already problem-ridden world.

Closing her eyes, she tried to remember exactly what she had seen when the man left the café. There was nothing that told her it was Frank, but there was nothing that told her it couldn't have been, either.

If it had been Frank, why hadn't he stopped to face her? When he'd come after her in the barn, he'd made it clear that he hated her—and it was his wish that she died. Yet this person had seen her and run. He hadn't wanted her to be able to identify him.

Maybe Frank had learned his lesson in court last time. Maybe he hadn't wanted her to be able to identify him. Yet the little knot in her gut told her that if Frank ever came after her again, he wouldn't simply just try to kill her with fire. He would stand there and make sure that he watched her burn. He'd never let her live.

She swallowed back the wave of nausea that passed over her.

It couldn't be Frank threatening everyone. It just couldn't be.

But that didn't leave her with any more answers. They needed to figure out who was threatening them before anything else happened or someone else got hurt.

Her thoughts moved to Sarah.

Colter had tried to convince her again and again that Sarah wouldn't want to hurt anyone, and he'd made a good point, but that didn't take her off the list of suspects. The perfect way to have everyone point the fingers away from her was to start a fire in her own store. Maybe she had wanted Whitney to spot her as she left through the back door—maybe she had worn the hat and coat in order to look masculine, all in an effort to throw off the investigation.

She had accused Whitney of starting the fire back in Kentucky in an attempt to get insurance money. Had Sarah gotten that idea because she herself was planning on doing exactly that—defrauding an insurance company?

She wouldn't have to worry about money anymore.

On the other hand, there were plenty of other people out there who hated the ranch and the people who worked on it—none more so than William Poe, the county tax appraiser. Maybe he had a hand in all of this. Lately, every time something bad had happened at the ranch, it could be traced to some kind of string he had pulled—not that any of it could be proved. He was a smart man—and Wyatt had said whoever was the maker of the bombs had been smart.

At least smart enough not to get caught.

She climbed down from the step stool and checked her work. The garland hung in graceful arcs and the red poinsettias the florist had brought were scattered around the barn, adding drops of color in the forest of brown, green and white.

"Do you guys need help with the tree?" she asked, making her way over to Colter and Merle.

Colter had a guilty smile as he looked over at her, and he slipped his dad a look that made her wonder what they were talking about before she had interrupted.

Merle handed her a box of red ornaments. "Here you go. If you want, you can put these up. I need to go check on Mother anyway. She was going to call the bartenders and make sure that everything was in order."

She took the box of ornaments and started to put them one by one on the spruce. The thing had to be at least twenty feet tall, as the angel's wings were almost grazing the ceiling. Something about the tree, maybe it was the mere size of the thing, reminded her of the Capitol Christmas Tree. It certainly would have done the nation proud.

"How's Lassie doing?" Colter asked, motioning toward the little dog that was sitting in the open door of the barn, looking at her.

"She's good. Got her a bath and a brushing. Now she thinks we're besties," she said, walking over and giving the dog a scratch behind the ears.

Now that the animal was clean and not in the arms of its owner, it didn't look like a rat creature. In fact, she had grown to think it almost cute in its awkwardness. If anything, she could relate to the poor creature. It had fallen and required the world to come to its rescue, and even with its fur matted and shivering and quaking, those around it had come to care for it.

She lifted the dog into her arms and carried it back to the tree, setting it down on the tree skirt as though it was a present. Milo came prancing in and, seeing the little dog, made his way over to lie down next to her. The pup they had likened to Lassie was no more than a fourth the size of Milo, and next to him looked like little more than a month-old puppy, but what she lacked in size she made up for in personality as she stood up and made her way between Milo's paws and forced him to move to accommodate her.

"It looks like he found himself a girlfriend," Colter said, motioning to the pups.

"That kind of thing seems to be catching," she teased, moving closer to him and giving him a quick peck on the cheek.

"Are you saying that you're my girlfriend?" He

gave her a look of surprise, like he couldn't believe that she had suddenly changed her mind about their having more than just a physical relationship.

"If you play your cards right," she teased, even though the only thing she really wanted was to jump into his arms and relive their night of lovemaking.

His touch had made her come alive again. It had made her want to forget everything about her past and what had happened, and it had even managed to dull the reemerging fears that had come after the fire. Though it had seemed impossible, he made her whole again.

There was the sound of a truck rattling to a stop in front of the barn, pulling her from her thoughts. The dogs lifted their noses, taking in the scent of something she couldn't quite make out.

"Who do you think that is?" she asked.

Colter shrugged. "No idea," he said, putting the last ornament from his box on the tree and dropping the box in the nearly empty crate.

She followed him outside. Backed up to the front of the barn was a large truck pulling a trailer. Strapped to the trailer was an industrial-sized black grill. The driver stepped out of the truck.

"Hey, Mayor Thomas," Colter said, but he had a look of confusion on his face. "What are you doing here?"

"Your brother told me that you were in a bit of a bind thanks to last night's fire. I had a grill sitting around, thought it might come to some good use around here."

"Wyatt called you?" Colter asked.

The mayor nodded. "He's a good man, as are you. It's the least I can do after all the years you and your brother have devoted to the town. Without men like you, and a ranch like this, it would be hard to keep our town afloat."

She couldn't help wondering if the mayor was using this chance to do goodwill in order to make a run for reelection, but his motivations didn't matter. All that mattered was that he was here, doing the right thing when they really could use the help.

"Thank you, Mayor," she said, shaking the man's hand in appreciation.

"Unfortunately, we don't have anything to go on it," Colter said, motioning up toward the grill.

The mayor turned toward the road. A line of cars made their way toward them over the cattle guard and parked in the gravel lot.

She recognized several of the men: the owner of the local bar called the Dog House, the grocery store owner and even the town's main butcher. There were also several people she didn't know. One by one, the men and women made their way to the barn, all carrying boxes full of meats and cheeses, fruits, nuts and premade little quiches. There was even one box full of chocolates.

With all the activity, Merle and Eloise had come

outside. Eloise was standing on her front porch, covering her mouth in shock.

"Oh, my goodness…" Eloise said, her eyes brimming with tears as she walked over to them. "What did you all do?"

The boxes of food kept coming until the tack room of the barn was nearly full.

Mayor Thomas smiled. "Mrs. Fitzgerald, your boy told us what you all were facing. We want you to know how much you and this ranch means to this town. Over the years, you and your family have given so much to this community. It's time that we return the favor."

"Oh, my… You all… You all didn't have to go to all this trouble. We…" Eloise said, emotions making her voice crack as she fumbled to find the right words.

"We wanted to," Mayor Thomas said. "More, we are going to make this the best Yule Night celebration that Dunrovin Ranch has ever seen."

A tear slipped down Eloise's cheek and a lump lodged in Whitney's throat as she watched the beautiful scene unfold in front of her. It was moments like these that gave her hope there were people out there who wanted to do the right thing—especially when those who wished them ill were looming just over the horizon.

Even with all the love in the air and the joy that filled her heart, there was something inside her that told her not was all as it seemed. Something didn't fit. Maybe it was her history, maybe it was her somewhat cynical ways, but Whitney couldn't let the little niggle of concern stop from pulling at her.

Maybe it was just that once everything started to go right in her life, the world had a way of crashing around her. This one time, she held the hope the world would wait—and for once people would continue to prove to be mostly good and her dreams of a bright future could continue to persevere.

Chapter Twenty

Fifteen minutes before the party was scheduled to begin, the parking lot of the ranch was full. The officers who had volunteered to help keep an eye out for anything that could compromise the party had been forced outside to direct traffic to park along the roads and anywhere they could safely get a car in and out of the snow. Wyatt and Gwen stood near the doors with a few of the off-duty officers, talking.

His mother and one of the ranch hands were standing by the front door of the barn and taking donations and money as guests started to make their way in. The country Christmas music echoed out of the barn as it mixed with the cacophony of voices coming from within. Everything was perfect, all the way down to the Christmas lights they had strung around the loft door and the peak of the barn. The blanket of snow made the multicolored lights a natural kaleidoscope, and the effect cast the place in a glow that reminded him of a Hallmark card.

The guests were all talking about how beautiful

the decorations were as they waited in line to get in the doors.

The scent of cooking meats wafted toward him from near the front doors, making his mouth water.

Everything about tonight would go great. It just had to. Something this perfect couldn't go wrong.

His mother waved him over to the line. "I just got a phone call," she said, excitement filling every syllable. "Your brother Rainier… They granted him parole. He'll be home next week."

He hadn't seen his brother since he had gone to prison. Though his mother was excited, he couldn't decide how he felt—Rainier had sworn up and down he had been unjustly sentenced, but there had been no denying he had assaulted the man. Maybe it was time Colter let bygones be bygones—just so long as when Rainier got home he could prove to them all he really had turned over a new leaf and was going to make choices not only good for him, but good for the family, as well.

Things were finally starting to go right; he would hate it if his brother's return also made his old troubles return.

"That's great, Mom," he said, giving her a hug.

His mother gripped him tight, squeezing him as she had done when he was a child, but she no longer seemed to have the strength she'd been full of back then. It was as if, over the last month or so, she had grown older.

"And he'll be home just in time for Christmas.

We'll have the whole family here. Waylon, Wyatt, you..." She fanned her face as though she were trying to hold back tears. "This is proving to be the best year. After everything that has happened, it's a miracle."

He glanced over at Whitney. She was smiling, but he could see a darkness in her eyes. He couldn't blame her for not trusting the world around them. She had been through hell and back. If he got a chance tonight, he would make it his personal goal to make her truly light up again—no matter what it took.

He gave her his best sexy smile, a smile that he hoped would tell her exactly what he had on his mind. As she looked over at him, her cheeks reddened and she looked away to one of the guests standing at their table.

The wind rustled the edge of her dress as she bent over to hand the guest a drink ticket, exposing her black panty hose high on her thigh.

Yes, he'd definitely have to see those later.

COLTER WAS IN rare form tonight and Whitney watched as he made his way into the barn with a man whom he had introduced to her as an old friend from his high school days. It wouldn't have surprised her if he knew almost every one of the hundreds of people who filled the barn and now had started to spill out into the yard and collect under the heat lamps they had set up.

It seemed surreal that just that morning there had

been talks about canceling the party. So many people were here, expressing their hopes and good wishes for the ranch and all who worked, lived and played there. One of the guests had even talked to Eloise about running the story on the nightly news.

Hopefully something like this, something that showed the community's true soul, would go viral.

Eloise nodded toward her. "Would you mind going and getting my camera? It's in my office. I would love to get some more pictures for our website. I want to make sure to publicly thank everyone who came tonight."

She made her way across the yard, passing by the husband and wife who had left her with Lassie. She smiled at them, but they pretended not to notice her, as though she wasn't worthy of being recognized as human just because she was a simple staff member.

The idea of having to give the dog back to them made her want to go get the poor little thing and dognap it until they were gone and the animal was safe. Yet, no matter how much she wanted to keep the animal, it wasn't hers.

Wasn't hers to keep… The thought turned her mind toward Colter. She had teased him about their relationship and what it could be and what she longed for it to be, but just like the pup, some things just couldn't be. Some things just weren't meant to be hers.

She walked through the quiet house, feeling strange that the place could be so full of silence when the barn, not even a few hundred yards away, was so full of noise. It was almost lonely. After grabbing the camera from the shelf in Eloise's office and being careful to avoid looking at anything on her desk, Whitney walked to the kitchen to get a quick drink of water before going back to the party.

It was nice to just be alone for a moment and to let her mind wander as she thought of all the things that had happened over the past few days. It shouldn't have surprised her how much a life could change in a matter of hours, yet it did. Perhaps what surprised her this time was how something so positive could all come from someone's evil deeds. It was almost as if the universe was finally trying to make up for some of what she had been through.

She took a sip of water, setting the glass beside the kitchen sink. There was a ripple of orange and a sparkle of red on the condensation on the kitchen window, catching her eye.

Outside, the toolshed had fingers of flames running up its siding, searing the wood. She grabbed the fire extinguisher from under the kitchen sink and rushed outside. As she looked down to pull the pin, she realized that she was still holding the camera and she dropped it in the snow.

She pulled the pin on the extinguisher as she drew close to the fire. Looking up, she stared at the orange tips of the flames. How did she always find herself near the inferno when all she wanted to do was find peace?

"Stop. Right. There," a man said from somewhere behind her.

She turned. Standing in the shimmering light was a man. His dark hair was greasy and matted against one side of his head and in his hand was a wooden baseball bat.

"Daryl? What are you doing here?" she asked, trying to stop the fear that was curdling the blood in her veins. Though the man looked slightly mad, he couldn't have come here with the intention of doing her any harm. She barely knew him. "Did Merle hire you for the party?" She tried to sound nonchalant.

The man laughed, the sound maniacal and edged with danger. "You stupid woman."

"Daryl…" she said. Edging away from him, she lifted the fire extinguisher and pointed it toward him. "What are you doing?"

He smiled at her and in the fire's light his smoke-stained teeth looked nearly brown. With the reflection of the flames in his eyes, he was almost the picture of what she had always imagined the Devil looked like.

"What are you gonna do with that thing?" he asked, pointing toward the extinguisher in her hands. "You gonna try to spray me to death?"

She raised it higher like a club. "If you take one more step toward me, I'll show you exactly what I'm going to do."

He laughed again, tilting his head back with mirth. "It's too bad that things have to play out this way. But one by one, I'm going to make sure that everyone in this place gets what's coming to them."

"Are you the one who left the note?"

His teeth glittered and a bit of spittle had worked its way out of the corner of his mouth. "If you were smart, you would have listened to my warning. You would have run. So if anyone is really at fault here, it's you. You are so arrogant. Just like the rest of them. It's no wonder you love Colter. He's just like you."

"But Wyatt said you helped him... Everyone here likes you. You're friends with Merle. Why would you want to do any of these people harm?"

He rushed at her, swinging the bat. The wooden bat connected with the metal tank in her hands as she held it up to block his swing. It made a loud twang as it connected. She hoped that someone in the parking lot or in the yard had heard the sound. Maybe they would see the smoke that had started to rise from the toolshed.

"Help!" she screamed.

She thrust the extinguisher at the man, but he simply jumped out of the way with a laugh. Something fell out of his back pocket and landed in the snow at his feet.

"Do you really think you can hurt me?" he asked.

She stared down at the little black object. He swung again, and as if in slow motion, the toe of her boot stuck in something in the snow, sending her sprawling.

The bat connected with her ribs, and pain shot

through her chest so sharp and ragged that she was sure she would lose consciousness.

She rolled over, tearing at the snow as she tried to get out of the man's range. But it was too late. Her luck had run out.

This was it.

He swung. The bat connected with her temple. The love, the pain, the Christmas lights and the orange fingers of the fire—it all disappeared.

Chapter Twenty-One

As the deejay picked a slow song, couples emerged from the crowd and took their places on the dance floor. They moved as if they were all part of a machine, each couple a little cog in the party. Colter smiled as he watched them. It was all going so well even Wyatt and his friends had begun to relax and now a few were drinking beers as they stood guard by the doors.

Thankfully their fears hadn't been realized. Perhaps whoever was behind the fire at Sarah's had gotten spooked and finally come to the point that they were ready to stop—maybe it was just some dumb kid behind it, a kid who thrived on crazy self-righteous ideals that had not yet been tested by the world.

He glanced around the barn, looking for Whitney. Sarah was standing beside his mother. Her blond hair was pulled tight, making the tired lines around her eyes look stretched and harsher in the thin light of the barn. He made his way over to the women.

"Hi, ladies. Sarah," he said, with an acknowledging tip of his head. "I'm surprised you came. How are you feeling today?"

She shrugged. "Still in shock… I just can't believe it."

"Did the fire inspector come by today?"

Sarah nodded. "He was with a detective. They found what they called incendiary devices. From what they said, someone used some kind of accelerant to start the fire."

"Do they have any idea who may have been behind it?" he asked, even though he was more than aware, thanks to Wyatt, of how little information they were going on.

"No, but when they find out who's behind this…" From the look on her face, it was no idle threat.

"Don't worry, Sarah. I know they're working to get to the bottom of this." He left it vague, but his mother gave him a look that told him he shouldn't tell her exactly how far all this went. "We're all doing our best to make sure that the perpetrator gets the justice they deserve and that no one else gets hurt."

A cold wind kicked up and blew through the open door of the barn, making goose bumps rise on his arms even though he had thought himself warm.

Sarah snorted in derision. "Everything I ever worked for is gone. My future. My home. Everything. Unless the person behind this dies, they will hardly get what they deserve."

The way she spoke made her sound nearly as dangerous as the person who had struck the match, and from the look on his mother's face, Sarah had made her just as uncomfortable as she had made him.

"Have you ladies seen Whitney?" he asked in an attempt to help change the subject.

Sarah set her jaw at the mention of Whitney's name.

"I sent her to the house," his mother said, ignoring the displeasure on Sarah's face. "I wanted her to get the camera. It must have been fifteen minutes or so ago."

"You haven't seen her again?"

His mother shook her head. "She's probably around, taking pictures. I was hoping we could use them to market this for next year."

He could tell that she was trying to meter the excitement in her voice, but she was pleased with the turnout.

"We are lucky to have such great support," he said. "You know, Sarah, maybe we could do something here to help raise money to rebuild your café. I'm sure everyone would be interested in helping. There's been all kinds of talk about what we could do."

She gave him a weak smile. "I had insurance. Hopefully it will come through. I don't want to take handouts."

Just when he thought he didn't like her, Sarah surprised him with her resilience.

"Just a thought," he said, patting her on the shoulder.

"Actually," his mother said, taking the lead, "it

wouldn't be a bad idea. We could even do it when the café gets up and running again. Like an open house kind of thing."

"You mean *if* I get up and running again."

"Well, we're going to need our caterer for future events," his mother said.

"If you ladies will excuse me," he said, motioning outside, thankful that some of the darkness had seemed to lift from their conversation. "I'm going to go check on Whit."

The women were so wrapped up in their plans that his mother simply waved him off. He almost could have sworn that, from his mother's playful grin, she had done it on purpose to let him off the hook. He couldn't have been more thankful. Though he liked Sarah and felt sorry for all that she was going through, he didn't want to get wrapped up in her business, out of loyalty for Whitney.

Maybe someday the two women could be friends, but he wasn't about to hold his breath in hopes that that day would be soon to arrive.

Outside, people were huddled near the heat lamps, laughing and talking as they drank their warm mulled wine and bottles of beer. Whitney wasn't anywhere to be seen. And though he asked around, no one had seemed to have seen her.

He made his way through the yard. The winter air smelled like wood smoke and cinnamon, sharp and earthy. He glanced around for the campfire, but there was none. The aroma of smoke had to have been coming from the woodstove in the ranch house. He'd always loved that scent, but something about it tonight was off.

He waved as he made his way past the crowds of people and to the ranch house. The front door was open, and as he slipped inside he was met with uncomfortable silence.

"Whit? You in here?"

There was no answer.

The lights were off throughout the house, all except the kitchen, and he made his way to the back. There was a glass of water sitting next to the sink, and a single droplet slipped down the edge from the pink stain of lipstick on its rim. If that was hers, she had to be close. He called her name again, but again there was no answer.

He walked over to the sink and picked up the glass. It was still cold. The doors of the cupboard under the sink were open and he clicked them shut. Odd.

A flicker of red caught his eye and he peered out the window. In the backyard, the toolshed was completely engulfed in flames.

He rushed outside and toward the fire. Halfway to the shed, lying in the snow, was his mother's camera.

His body went numb.

"Whitney!" he yelled, terror rippling through his voice. He knew she wouldn't answer.

He rushed toward the flames, and as he grew near he was met with the red stain of droplets in the snow.

To the left of them was a fire extinguisher. She must have come out here in hopes that she could stop the fire's advance. But what had happened to her? Where was she?

The snow around him had been trampled down, and a few feet from him there was a splotch of blood nearly the size of one's head. He carefully stepped around the mark, but as he came closer he could see a set of footprints in the snow and what looked like drag marks, leading directly to the back of the toolshed.

He ran next to the marks. Around the corner, behind the shed, lay Whitney. Her hair was matted with blood that had started to spill out into the snow around her, making her look as though she lay in a red, otherworldly cloud.

He rushed to her side and pressed his fingers against her neck. There was the faint but reassuring thump of her heartbeat. She was still alive, but just barely.

"Baby, wake up." He brushed her hair back from her face. He needed her to wake up. He needed to know she was okay.

On the side of her head was a large lump and the blood poured from a cut at its center. She didn't open her eyes.

He couldn't leave her here, not this close to the fire. Not with a killer on the loose. But he couldn't get the help he needed without doing something.

He pulled his phone from his pocket and dialed

Wyatt. He answered on the first ring and his voice sounded happy as he answered.

"Wyatt... There's a killer on the loose. They attacked Whitney. Toolshed is on fire. Call it in. We're going to need help."

Chapter Twenty-Two

Hate filled him. For the first time in his life, he wanted to kill.

Colter slipped his fingers between Whitney's as he waited for the ambulance to arrive.

"It's going to be okay," he said, not sure whether or not she could hear him. "Help's on the way. You're going to be okay. You are safe now."

He never should have left her alone. He shouldn't have let the party happen. He shouldn't have put anyone in this kind of danger. He had been so stupid. So naive. So idiotic to trust that for one night the world and the evil within it wouldn't tear away at this place and the people he loved.

They should have listened and taken it more seriously, but no. He had been too wrapped up in the needs and wants of his heart. He had been blinded by love. Love had kept him from being objective and from the one thing he had vowed he would do—protect the people he cared about.

In that moment, it was like he was a scared kid

again, sitting outside the fire department, his world destroyed.

Wyatt rushed to the backyard, running toward him with two men at his heels. "What happened?"

Colter shook his head. "We have to find whoever is behind this. They're here. Somewhere."

A few steps from him, Wyatt stopped. There was the crunch of something under his foot. Reaching down, he picked up a black cell phone and wiped the snow clean from its screen. Though the glass was cracked, it came to life.

"Is this hers?" Wyatt asked, holding it up for him to see.

There was a picture of a big rig as the phone's wallpaper screen.

Colter shook his head. "Her phone's pink."

"Is she…alive?" Wyatt said, motioning toward her.

"For now. Did you call 911?"

Wyatt nodded. "They should be here anytime."

The deputies who had followed Wyatt rushed to Whitney's side, and one started to take her vitals. "Her pulse is sixty-eight," the man to his right said, like Colter could take some measure of comfort from the fact that the number was normal.

Yet, no matter how normal the number, it didn't change the fact that she wasn't regaining consciousness—or that she might never come back to him.

The thought made a lump lodge in his throat. How was it that when he finally found the one woman in the world whom he wanted to share his future with, the world stole her from him? Perhaps he was never meant to have anything good in his life. Perhaps he was going to be forever cursed.

Wyatt tapped on the phone, pulling up the most recent calls.

There, at the top of the list, was the name William.

Wyatt hit the redial button, putting the call on speaker.

The phone rang. On the second ring, someone picked up.

"Hey, brother. How's the party going?" William Poe asked, his voice souring the air around them. When Colter didn't answer right away, William said, "Daryl?"

Brother? He'd had no idea. From what Wyatt had told him, Daryl was from Canada and they didn't share the same last name. He and William must have only been half brothers, but he'd never heard mention of them even knowing one another before.

"Daryl? You there? What happened?" William pressed. "Did you do as I asked? No one caught you, did they? It's vital that they don't find out we are connected in any way."

Colter reached over and clicked off the phone.

He and his half brother were going to pay for what they had done.

Wyatt reached over and gripped his shoulder. "It's going to be all right. You need to stay with me."

He jerked out of his brother's grip. "If she dies, I will kill William and his damn brother with my bare hands."

Wyatt motioned toward his friends. "We need to find Daryl Bucket. Put out a BOLO. If he's smart, by now he's left the ranch, but he couldn't have gotten far. And one of you needs to go make sure everyone in the barn is safe. For now, let's try and keep everyone inside, but let's not reveal anything. We don't want to cause panic. Calm. Collected. In control. Go."

The two men took off in the direction of the barn.

Though Colter knew he could trust the men to do what had to be done, he couldn't help the feeling of dread and disdain that crept through him. They wouldn't find Daryl. No one would. If Daryl was anything like his brother, he'd be more slippery than an eel and harder to catch.

"You go clear the house," Colter said, motioning toward Wyatt. "We need to make sure that he hasn't planted anything." He looked toward the house as thoughts of the Molotov cocktails came to mind.

Wyatt nodded. "Are you sure you'll be okay?"

"I've got her. We just need to make sure that, like you said, everyone else stays safe. He's going to be out for the family. For all we know, he came after her first in hopes of creating a diversion so he could go after everyone else. You need to make sure that doesn't happen."

"I have my phone if you need anything." He turned to go.

"Wait."

Wyatt stopped, turning back.

"Leave me a gun," Colter said.

Wyatt frowned at him. "Why do you need a gun?"

"If I find Daryl…"

Wyatt shook his head. "We have to stop him. You're right about that. And he needs to pay for what he's done. But you need to stay true to who you are—they win if you sink to their levels. We're Fitzgeralds. We're better than them."

Right now, though he could hear the logic in his brother's words, he couldn't agree with them. Sometimes the right thing wasn't the easy thing. And what could have been better than stripping the world of Daryl's kind of filth? Anyone who wanted to hurt a woman deserved to die.

Wyatt took off, disappearing around the corner of the house and out into the road as he made his way toward the barn and stables.

Whitney moaned.

"Whit, baby, it's going to be okay," Colter said, running his hand over her hair. "We're going to find Daryl. He's going to pay for what he's done."

Her eyelashes fluttered as though she was struggling to regain consciousness.

"It's okay, baby. You're going to be okay," he cooed, but as he watched her struggle, rage filled him.

If only he hadn't left her side, this wouldn't have

happened. He should have been there to protect her and to stop this from happening. He had known there was danger out there.

"No matter what happens, baby, I love you," he said, rubbing his thumb over the soft skin of her cheek.

Her eyelashes fluttered, but once again she lost the battle for consciousness and her head rolled to the side.

It wasn't how he'd wanted this to go, any of this. All he'd wanted was to build a life, a future with the woman he loved.

Why did the world have to be so cruel?

"Isn't that sweet?" a man said, his voice hoarse and crackling like that of a smoker.

Colter looked up, in the direction of the fire and the man's voice. Standing behind the toolshed was a man dressed all in black. His face was blotched with bits of soot and sweat and his dark hair was matted against the side of his face with streaks of drying blood. In his hand was a bat, the end of it covered in crimson drips.

"Go to hell, Daryl," Colter said, slowly rising to his feet.

The man laughed. "Oh, no, that's where you and your family will be going. And as soon as you all are there, my brother and I are going to take your ranch and everything you care about and burn it to the ground."

"Like hell you are," Colter said, taking a step toward the man.

"Take one more step and you will look like that girl there." Daryl raised the bat, readying to strike. "You should have seen her go down. It was just like a bag of potatoes."

On the ground at Colter's feet was a dented fire extinguisher. He knelt down and picked it up, not taking his gaze off the maniac standing near the flames.

Daryl laughed. "You're one hell of a firefighter if you think that little thing is going to put out those flames," he said, motioning toward the toolshed. One side of the building was starting to list dangerously toward him.

"I have no intention of putting out the fire." This time he was only going to be a fighter—life or death, he was going to find out and he was going to give everything he had…everything for his family and for Whitney.

He lunged toward Daryl, who swung wildly at him with the bat. Colter used the extinguisher to block the man's shot, and when it connected with the metal it made a twang and vibrated like a bell in his hands. Before Daryl could pull the bat back, Colter reached down and took hold of it. He pulled it, but Daryl wouldn't let go.

In one swift motion, Colter lifted the fire extinguisher and swung it at the man's head. It connected with his temple, sending blood spattering over the steadily melting snow.

Daryl staggered and swung the bat drunkenly. He stumbled over his own feet, listing toward the tool-shed. He moved as though he was trying to avoid the flames, but his body disobeyed and he crashed into the building.

Embers careened into the air around him and the small shed collapsed around the man, engulfing him in its superheated grip.

For a second, Colter stood watching the flames. He could let the man die. There would be no reprisal. Only William Poe would come after him, and he was already undoubtedly a target on that man's list.

The smoke curled into the night air.

Wyatt had been right. If he let the man die, if he stood by and did nothing, he would be no better than the men who tried to do them harm. In fact, he would be just like his own biological father—abandoning the one thing that made him who he was and gave him purpose, in order to fulfill the unjust and dark desires of the wolf inside him.

He pushed back a burning two-by-four, grabbed Daryl's foot and pulled.

Colter was, and would always be, a good man. A man who believed in the goodness and redeemability of people—even those who had wronged the people he loved.

Chapter Twenty-Three

Ten stitches and two days later, Whitney was finally starting to feel better. She wasn't seeing the flames every time she closed her eyes, and the smell of smoke was finally starting to dissipate from the ranch. Colter had been great, and even when they had kept her at the hospital overnight for observation, he hadn't left her side.

He was on the phone with Wyatt, and from what she could make out, Daryl was still under guard at the hospital. He was in critical condition because of his burns, but in his pain-medication-induced honesty he had confessed to starting the fire at Sarah's café. If he recovered, he would head to jail. She should have felt some degree of relief that he was going to pay for what he'd done to her. Yet, as she ran her fingers over the bandage on her temple, the only comfort she could find was that she had Colter. They would protect each other from the world.

The door to the office opened and the hoity-toity

husband and wife made their way in. The woman was wearing a different pair of stilettos, equally high and equally as unpractical in the knee-deep snow and ice outside.

"Hello. How was your stay?" Whitney said, welcoming them with as much warmth as she could muster.

The wife wouldn't look at her, but the husband nodded. "It was very nice. We were just hoping to check out and pick up Francesca."

"So that's the dog's name," she said with a sad laugh as she glanced over at Lassie and Milo, who were currently snuggling together on Milo's bed. She'd forgotten it completely.

The woman glanced over at the dog and snapped her fingers. "Come, Francesca."

The dog looked up at her for a moment, then pushed its face under Milo's armpit as though it could hide from the woman.

"I guess she's not wanting to go home," Whitney said, trying not to sound as brokenhearted as she felt.

"That's ridiculous," the woman snapped. "She's just not listening." She clapped her hands, the sound as shrill as the woman in the small space of the office.

The dog only pushed its way farther under Milo's front leg.

"Come. Here. Dog," the woman commanded, pointing at the floor at her feet.

Watching the woman in action, Whitney thought

it was really no wonder that the dog wanted nothing to do with her.

The dog started to shake under Milo.

The woman walked over and reached down to pick up the pup. Milo looked up at her, and with a lift of his lip, such as Whitney had never seen, he snarled at her. The woman recoiled.

"Did you see that thing?" she said, pointing to Milo. "Your dog was going to bite me."

And what was more, Whitney couldn't blame him. "I think they have fallen in love. He doesn't want to see her go."

"And neither do we," Colter said, clicking off his phone. "You know, if you'd like, you are more than welcome to leave Francesca here. We promise to give her a good home, one full of care and love."

Whitney smiled at him. "Absolutely. We'd love to have her."

The woman frowned. "But she's mine."

Her husband shrugged. "Don't worry, love. I'll just buy you another. One that is better trained this time."

"Fine," the woman said. "But next time, I want a prettier one." She pushed her way outside as the husband paid their bill.

He didn't leave a tip.

Colter laughed as soon as the couple was safely outside and away. "Wow. Is that what you have to put up with every day?"

"Most are better than them, but hey, at least we

got something good from it." She motioned toward the dog. "Come here, Lassie."

The dog untangled itself from Milo and came hopping over, licking her hand as she reached down to give it a scratch behind the ears.

"I'm sure we can't be half as happy as she is," Colter said, looking at the dog. "And hey, we have our first animal together."

She smiled. "You're definitely the kind of guy I want to own a dog with."

Colter chuckled. "I'll take that as a high compliment. And if you're open to dog ownership, I'm taking it you're going to stay?"

"Well, if I am invited, I just may," she teased.

"Hmm. I guess an invitation could be extended. After all, you went out of your way to take down a killer."

"More like I stood in the way, but hey... I'll play the hero." She walked to the door and looked out at the old blue pickup, complete with BF Goodrich All-Terrain tires, which had belonged to Daryl Bucket. "Are they going to come tow that thing away?" she asked, motioning to the truck.

"Wyatt said he'd send someone out later today and they'd take it to the county's impound lot."

She didn't care, as long as she never had to see that thing, or Daryl, again.

"Why don't we get out of here for a little bit? All the other guests are checked out, right?"

"Yeah, that would be great." It would be nice to get out of the office that still smelled of the guest's perfume.

Colter slipped on his coat and she followed suit. They made their way outside and to the barn.

She watched Colter as he lifted the bale of hay and threw it into the wheelbarrow. Breaking off a couple of flakes, he took them to the mare closest to them and dropped them into her stall. There were still the cedar shavings from the party on the floor, and the Christmas tree stood at the end of the barn, not moving now until the holidays were over.

Lassie and Milo made their way into the barn and sat by the door, keeping them company and watching on with approval.

The horse nickered in thanks and started to munch on the hay he'd given her. Whitney walked over to the wheelbarrow and grabbed a couple of flakes and dropped them into the next stall. Clark stuck his head out and she gave him a scratch at the top of his head. He ignored the hay she had thrown in, instead choosing to take in more attention.

"You're a little stinker," she said, smiling at the horse.

"Is that what you think of me now—I'm a stinker?" Colter teased, though from his smile she could tell that he knew she was talking to the gelding.

"I would use much stronger words for you, Colter Fitzgerald."

He got an innocent look on his face. "Who, me? The man who saved your life?"

"How about I just call you God's gift to women?" she said with a derisive snort.

He smirked as he pointed toward himself. "I guess you could call me that or Superman or Firefighter Extraordinaire. Better yet, you could call me your husband."

He said it like it was just another name and he hadn't just made her entire body clench with excitement.

"What?" she whispered. "Why would I call you that?"

His wicked smile grew larger. "Well, you don't have to." He walked over to the wheelbarrow. Tucked into the bale of hay was a small black velvet box. He picked it up and knelt down on his knee in front of her.

She cupped her hands over her mouth.

"Whitney Barstow, I know we hadn't talked about this, and that it's a bit impulsive, but there are some things in life that you just *know*. I know that I love you. I know that I want to spend the rest of our lives together."

"But…what about my past?" she said. "About Daryl and William?"

"What about it? Them?" He looked up at her. "We all have a past, and if anyone ever comes after you again, I promise that I will always be at your side and ready to protect you. I'm never going to let anyone hurt you again. Seeing you there…by the fire…"

She reached down and ran her fingers through his hair. "It's okay, Colter. That wasn't your fault. You couldn't have stopped that. Sometimes bad things just happen."

"Well, let's make a stand. Let's focus on the good. Let's get married and start the great," he said, clicking open the box.

Inside was a cushion-cut diamond ring set in white gold. It was simple and elegant.

"It's one of a kind, just like you," he said, smiling up at her.

"Oh, Colter…" She leaned down and kissed his lips.

"Is that a yes?" he said, his lips brushing against her as he spoke.

She nodded, throwing her arms around his neck. "Always… I love you, Colter Fitzgerald."

He held her, box still in his hand. "I love you, too. I always will."

She let go of him and he slipped the ring onto her finger.

Clark threw his head and whinnied at them from his stall.

"It looks like the little stinker is excited, too," Whitney said, staring at the new ring on her finger. "You know…" She glanced over at the horse. "If we're going to have great new beginnings, you know what I want to do?"

Colter slipped his hand in hers. "What?"

She motioned toward Clark. "How about we go for a ride?"

"I thought you'd never ask." Colter picked her up and she wrapped her legs around him. She cupped his face in her hands and gave him a kiss and, with it, the silent promise that they would be together forever—and that she would love him until the end of time.

Just like his smile, their future looked merry and bright.

* * * * *

Can't get enough of Mystery, Montana?
Check out the previous titles in the series
from Danica Winters:

MS. CALCULATION
MR. SERIOUS

And don't miss the final book:

MS. DEMEANOR

Available December 2017
from Harlequin Intrigue!

COMING NEXT MONTH FROM

⊞ HARLEQUIN®

I N T R I G U E

Available November 21, 2017

#1749 ALWAYS A LAWMAN
Blue River Ranch • by Delores Fossen
Years ago, Jodi Canton and Sheriff Gabriel Beckett were torn apart by a shocking murder and false conviction. Can they now face the true killer and rekindle the love they thought they'd lost?

#1750 REDEMPTION AT HAWK'S LANDING
Badge of Justice • by Rita Herron
The murder of her father has brought Honey Granger back to her small Texas town, but despite his attraction to Honey the hot Sheriff Harrison Hawk has his own motives for looking into her father's death—the disappearance of his sister.

#1751 MILITARY GRADE MISTLETOE
The Precinct • by Julie Miller
Master Sergeant Harry Lockheart was the only survivor of the IED that killed his team—but he credits Daisy Gunderson's kind letters to his actual recovery. And now that he's finally met the woman of his dreams, he's not about to let a stalker destroy their dreams for the future.

#1752 PROTECTOR'S INSTINCT
Omega Sector: Under Siege • by Janie Crouch
When former police detective Zane Wales couldn't protect Caroline Gill, he left both her and the force behind, unable to face his failure. But now that a psychopath has Caroline in his sights, can Zane find the courage to face the past and protect the woman he loves still?

#1753 MS. DEMEANOR
Mystery Christmas • by Danica Winters
Rainier Fitzgerald manages to attract both a heap of trouble and the attention of his parole officer, Laura Blade, only hours after his release. Can the two of them crack the cold case on Dunrovin ranch or will Christmas be behind bars?

#1754 THE DEPUTY'S WITNESS
The Protectors of Riker County • by Tyler Anne Snell
Testifying against a trio of lethal bank robbers has drawn a target on Alyssa Garner's back, and the only man who can save her from the crosshairs is cop Caleb Foster, who harbors secrets of his own...

YOU CAN FIND MORE INFORMATION ON UPCOMING HARLEQUIN® TITLES, FREE EXCERPTS AND MORE AT WWW.HARLEQUIN.COM.

HICNM1117

Get 2 Free Books,
Plus 2 Free Gifts—

just for trying the Reader Service!

HARLEQUIN
INTRIGUE

HI17R

She had died here. Temporarily, anyway.

But she was alive now, and Jodi Canton could feel the nerves
just beneath the surface of her skin. With the Smith & Wesson
gripped in her hand, she inched closer to the dump site where
he had left her for dead.

There were no signs of the site now. Nearly ten years had
passed, and the thick Texas woods had reclaimed the ground.
It didn't look nearly so sinister dotted with wildflowers and a
honeysuckle vine coiling over it. No drag marks.

No blood.

The years had washed it all away, but Jodi could see it, smell
it and even taste it as if it were that sweltering July night when
a killer had come within a breath of ending her life.

The nearby house had succumbed to time and the elements,
too. It'd been a home then. Now the white paint was blistered,
several of the windows on the bottom floor closed off with
boards that had grayed with age. Of course, she hadn't expected
this place to ever feel like anything but the crime scene that it
had once been.

Considering that two people had been murdered inside.

Jodi adjusted the grip on the gun when she heard the footsteps. They weren't hurried, but her visitor wasn't trying to sneak up on her, either. Jodi had been listening for that. Listening for everything that could get her killed.

Permanently this time.

Just in case she was wrong about who this might be, Jodi pivoted and took aim at him.

"You shouldn't have come here," he said. His voice was husky and deep, part lawman's growl, part Texas drawl.

The man was exactly who she thought it might be. Sheriff Gabriel Beckett. No surprise that he had arrived, since this was Beckett land, and she'd parked in plain sight on the side of the road that led to the house. Even though the Becketts no longer lived here, Gabriel would have likely used the road to get to his current house.

"You came," Jodi answered, and she lowered her gun.

Muttering some profanity with that husky drawl, Gabriel walked to her side, his attention on the same area where hers was fixed. Or at least it was until he looked at her the same exact moment that she looked at him.

Their gazes connected.

And now it was Jodi who wanted to curse. Really? After all this time that punch of attraction was still there? She had huge reasons for the attraction to go away and not a single reason for it to stay.

Yet it remained.

Don't miss
ALWAYS A LAWMAN,
available December 2017 wherever
Harlequin® Intrigue books and ebooks are sold.

www.Harlequin.com

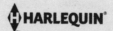